Christmas Past

A Ghostly Winter Tale

By the same author and illustrator:

Raven Wakes the World: A Winter Tale

Christmas Past

A Ghostly Winter Tale

By John Adcox
Illustrated by Carol Bales

The Story Plant
Studio Digital CT, LLC
P.O. Box 4331
Stamford, CT 06907

Text Copyright © 2021 by John Adcox
Illustrations Copyright © 2021 by Carol Bales

Story Plant hardcover ISBN-978-1-61188-312-1
Fiction Studio Books e-book ISBN-978-1-945839-56-6

Visit our website at www.TheStoryPlant.com

First Story Plant Printing: November 2021

Printed in the United States of America

Library of Congress Cataloging-in-Publication Data is available
Identifiers: LCCN 2021042461 (print) | LCCN 2021042462 (ebook)
Subjects: LCGFT: Christmas fiction. | Magic realist fiction. | Novels

For our families, blood and chosen

Foreword

In 2001, my dear friend Carol Bales (who later became my beloved wife) and I began the tradition of creating holiday gifts of story for our friends and family. I wrote a story; she created illustrations. We bound them by hand. At the time, our plan was to do a new one every year. *Raven Wakes the World*, the first of our stories, has already been rewriten and published, and should be available now in your favorite bookstore. *Raven Wakes the World* is a sort of mythic romance based on Inuit mythology.

This is the second story, originally titled *I'll Be Home for Christmas*. It is our take on a different sort of myth— the urban legend. I'd been working on a completely different story, and was in fact reading some of the opening pages to some writer friends over a pint at an Irish pub when the idea of tracking an urban legend back to its original source, and finding there a Christmas miracle, occurred to me. The lesson here, I suppose, is that Guinness and truly excellent fish and chips are an integral part of the creative process. In any case, I fell in love with the new idea at once, and the original story was never finished. *Hmmm.* Maybe next Christmas.

In addition to being retitled, this version has been rewritten and expanded extensively, incorporating some elements from the screenplay version (yes, this story is presently somewhere in development purgatory and, I hope, on its way to a screen, big or small). The movie version is rather different—Jessie is a doctor rather than a folklorist, but the heart is the same. Urban folklore varies as it spreads, after all. David and the Christmas ornament weren't in the original version; they were born in the screenplay.

Thanks once again to our many dear friends and family members for the blessings of their love and inspiration. Many thanks to James Lock, Bill Bridges, John Bridges, Ted Anderson, Sid "Bubba" Taylor, Zachary Steele, Jolie Simmons, Nancy Fletcher, Maryann Daves Lozano, and Andrew Greenberg for helping me polish this tale. Thanks to the teachers who taught me to write, including Judith Pritchett, Jim Meeks, and Christina Kaylor. Thanks to Paul Jenkins for polishing my English colloquialisms and checking my knowledge of soccer, er, I mean "football." Thanks to fellow authors Zachary Steele and Benji Carr for support and community, and to Neighborhood Church for giving this version of the tale a place to be born. I am grateful to Don Dudenhoeffer, Alice Neuhauser, and Irtaza Barlas—and the whole team at Gramarye Media—for being great people and business partners. Finally, I am forever grateful to Charles de Lint, Paul Brandon, and the late great Ray Bradbury and Lloyd Alexander for many kind words and much encouragement. Very special thanks to the great Lou Aronica and Peter Miller for pushing me to bring this story home, and in time for the winter holiday.

Most of all, thanks to Carol, love of my life.

Carol and I wish you and yours the happiest of Winter Holiday seasons, and safe and happy homecomings, no matter what, or who, home means to you.

"Myth is something that never happened, but is happening all the time."

— Sallistius, Greek poet

"It might seem unlikely that legends—urban legends at that—would continue to be created in an age of widespread literacy, rapid mass communications, and restless travel. A moment's reflection, however, reminds us of the many weird, fascinating, but unverified rumors and tales that so frequently come to our ears. The lack of verification in no way diminishes the appeal urban legends have for us. We enjoy them merely as stories, but we tend to at least half-believe them as possibly accurate reports. And the legends we tell, as with any folklore, reflect many of the hopes, fears, and anxieties of our times. . . . One of the great mysteries of folklore research is where oral traditions originate and who invents them. Most leads pointing to authors or original events lying behind urban legends have simply evaporated."

— Jan Harold Brunvand

"Facts interest me less than the trailing smoke of stories."
— Naomi Shihab Nye

1

The Vanishing Workday

I was in London when I first heard about Sam's ghost.

God knows I didn't have time to be following a ghost tale, no matter how intriguing it might sound. My tiny flat was filled to the rafters with books and notebooks full of research I'd gathered but not organized. They needed my attention desperately. The looming piles of research I hadn't yet begun to plow through were even more daunting. A forest of post-it notes covered every flat surface.

But I couldn't stop thinking about Sam.

Focus, Jessie girl, I commanded myself with my sternest inner voice. *Focus!*

It didn't help.

On the surface, Sam's ghost seemed to be a variant of the Vanishing Hitchhiker motif. You've heard it. Maybe somebody told it to you at an office party, or a pub, or around a campfire. Campfires are the best for stories. Anyway, a friend of a friend swears it's true. That's how urban legends work, you know. Someone picks up a hitcher on a dark and stormy night, only to have the passenger disappear before they reach the destination. When the driver asks around, he finds that the hitcher's description matches that of a daughter or a bride or a girlfriend who died years before. It's almost always a woman.

Except for Sam.

More, the details of Sam's story didn't seem to vary from report to report the way they should, not even subtly; only the dates and location changed. Well, the point where the story began changed. The ending did not. It's like the folk process hadn't touched it at all, and the tale was apparently at least sixty years old. That just shouldn't be. No, more than that. It *couldn't* be.

No, no. *No.*

I was approaching the lip of a rabbit hole again. I didn't have time. I was scheduled to go to Paris for research in just a few days; it was all arranged. If I came back with new data from the French libraries before I managed to sort what I'd already done, I'd have no hope. My dissertation would be lost forever, buried under an avalanche of unannotated paper and post-it notes. I didn't have time to eat, sleep, or even breathe, much less get distracted by something new, something that didn't have anything at all to do with my topic.

No matter that, unlike most urban legends, this one seemed to be a serial story—one that apparently continued, year to year, rather than simply being passed along by a friend of a friend, acquiring slight variations each time it's retold.

No matter that the latest episode actually seemed fresh, fresh and perhaps even local to London. Fresh enough that I might really be able to track down a genuine original source, at least for the latest variation, anyway.

No. Uh uh. I didn't have time. No matter that I might become one of the very few cultural anthropologists to actually track an urban legend to its source.

Besides, I wasn't even a cultural anthropologist yet—and I never would be if I didn't get a handle on the stupid dissertation. I wanted to be *Doctor* Jessie Malone. That meant I had to focus. I put a kettle for tea on the stove and, with effort, banished Sam's ghost from my thoughts. I had to finish my dissertation.

I'd promised David, after all. I'd promised him. A promise to my David is sacred.

My dissertation was supposed to be on variations of the Pleading Ghost story. You've probably heard that one, too. It goes rather like this:

A poor priest in London—it's usually London in the oldest variations; convenient, since that's where I happened to be researching it—is reading alone in his home one evening when he hears a knock at his door. Pulling on a robe over his dressing gown, he opens the door to find an old woman wearing rather outdated clothing, including a bonnet and shawl. It's almost always a bonnet and a shawl, even though they're not always black. But I'm being a scholar instead of a storyteller.

Anyway.

The frantic woman begs the priest to come with her, saying he is needed desperately. The priest resists, citing the cold, the snow, and the late hour. Perhaps he can come 'round tomorrow instead. The woman persists, and eventually the priest agrees. She gives him an address in Regent's Park, and he goes to dress and get a coat. The priest suffers a cold and miserable walk through the dark streets of the fog-bound city.

Later, he arrives at one of London's ritziest manors to find an elegant party in full swing. All of London's elite is present. Our priest knocks on the door, and a butler answers.

"Hello," says the shivering priest. He then gives his name—sometimes it's Mulligan, sometimes Gray, sometimes Johnson, or a dozen or more variant Irish, Scottish, Welsh, or English names. "I believe I'm wanted here," he says.

"Do you have an invitation, Father?" the butler asks curtly.

"No," says the priest, rather flustered. "But I was told I'm needed."

The butler escorts him to a small sitting room and presently returns with the master of the house, a very well-known and respected gentleman, usually a lord or a banker or something like that. The priest tells the gentleman what happened.

The gentleman claims that no one sent for a priest but asks our friend to describe his visitor. The priest does so, and a strange look crosses the gentleman's face.

And then, suddenly, the man starts weeping uncontrollably. As our friend the priest holds the sobbing man, he confesses a life of terrible crime and wickedness. The details always vary, but believe me, they're never pleasant.

The priest urges the man to confess and make his peace with God. The man does so, and the priest, convinced of the sincerity of his conversion, grants him absolution with a gentle smile and a touch to the bowed head. As he leaves, he admonishes the man to come to Mass in the morning. The man promises to do so, and the priest bids him good night.

The next day, of course, the man doesn't show. Concerned, the priest goes to visit him again. Once again, the butler answers, telling the priest that the master is dead.

"That can't be!" exclaims the priest. "I spoke to him just last night!"

"Alas," insists the butler, "the master died in his sleep."

17

Shocked, the priest asks to see the body that he might say a prayer for the man's soul. The butler agrees. When they reach the master's bedroom, the priest notices a portrait hanging on the wall and recognizes the woman who came to fetch him the night before.

"Who's that woman?" he asks.

"Why, that's the master's mother, Father," says the butler. "She died several years ago."

The tale always ends the same way. It was recorded in Philadelphia as early as 1951. Two different sources there claimed to have heard it in London from an acquaintance of the priest himself. A friend of a friend. Of course, both sources gave conflicting details and locations in the city.

I've found variations of the Pleading Ghost story all over the world, but for the most part, the trails all seem to lead back to London. I say "seem" because some variants were recorded in Paris at about the same time. Here in London, I'd found sources dating back to the 1800s. Some may be even older, but, well, again with the post-it notes and the piles of research I hadn't plowed through yet. I planned to start the next phase of my research in Paris at the first of the next week. My hope was to pin down a single origin for the tale—I truly wanted to be one of the very few to find and identify an actual original source.

That might not prove possible, of course, but it wouldn't be for a lack of sources. Seriously, I had piles of material to read through. I'd spent the morning at the British Library going through archived newspapers and magazines and I'd spent the balance of the day tracking down old journals and diaries. Now the fruits of my labor waited in tall, intimidating piles, bushels upon bushels of them, demanding my attention.

I yawned.

The teakettle whistled, startling me with its appropriately ghostly wail, but I turned it off without bothering to pour myself a cup. I couldn't face the thought of reading or, worse, trying to organize my notes and resources into something more or less manageable. I yawned again, more prodigiously. It would all still be there tomorrow. Still waiting for me. For better or for worse, the workday had vanished, leaving me even further behind. I washed off my makeup, brushed my teeth, and went to bed.

I didn't let myself think about Sam's ghost as I lay in my cold bed in the darkness. If I wasn't going to work, I needed to sleep.

"Go away, Sam," I said out loud. "Just take your pattern-breaking story and be gone. Leave me alone." I couldn't afford to be distracted by a new tale.

No matter how much it intrigued me.

I glanced at David's picture on my bedside table before I drifted off to sleep. "Goodnight, my love," I said, just as I said every night before sleep took me. "Miss you."

I said that to him every night. Goodnight. I always said it. I always said that, because I couldn't bring myself to say goodbye, not to David. Not ever.

2

The Pleading Father

I was lost in a dream about ghosts and priests and mile-high towers of precariously stacked books and multiplying post-its when the phone rang and shocked me awake. I was too dazed to think not to answer it.

"Hello?" I managed.

"Jessie? Is that you? Were you asleep?"

"No, Daddy. . . ." I don't know why I always feel compelled to lie when people wake me. I guess I don't want them to feel bad. I totally need to get past that.

"You sound dazed, baby girl."

"It's 2:00 a.m., Daddy."

"Oh! It's barely after dinnertime here in Alabama!"

"It's six hours later here, Daddy."

"Oh. Sorry, baby. I thought it was the other way." I hated when he called me baby.

"No, Daddy."

"I never can keep that straight."

"I know, Daddy. It's okay."

"Well, I know you need your rest, so I won't keep you. Your mother and I just wanted to talk about your arrangements for the holidays."

I sat up. Sleep fell away from me like a blanket. "What arrangements?"

"Well, when are you coming home for Christmas, baby?"

"Daddy, we talked about this. I can't come to Birmingham for Christmas. I've just got too much—"

"Not coming home for Christmas!"

I sighed and shifted the phone to my other hand. "Daddy, I can't. Please—"

"But Jess. Baby. It's Christmas. What'll I tell your brother and the kids? What'll I tell your mother, for Heaven's sake?"

"We talked about this, Daddy. I can't." *This is why he calls me in the middle of the night,* I fumed to myself. *He thinks if I'm too tired to argue, I'll cave.* "I can't," I said again, more firmly.

"But you love Christmas! You've always loved Christmas. You've always loved coming home for Christmas." I didn't answer. For too long a moment, there was no sound, just Daddy breathing on the other end. "We understand that you can't come home for the whole season, Thanksgiving and New Years and all, but we thought *surely* you'd be here on Christmas Day!"

"I can't come to Alabama, Daddy. Really. I . . . I just can't. That's all." *God. Not yet.*

"But it'll be good for you, you know. You've been co-cooning too long. We worry, you know. Especially after David . . . You know."

"The word is died, Daddy. I'm a grownup. You can say it."

I heard him take a breath and let it out slowly. "You shouldn't be alone, baby. You should be home. Home for Christmas."

"I'm not ready, Daddy. Not yet."

"So when, then?"

"Daddy, please. It's the middle of the night."

"Oh! Right. Okay. I'm sorry, baby. I never can keep that straight. We'll talk about it later, okay?"

"Okay. Good night, Daddy."

"Good night, baby. Love you."

"I love you, too, Daddy."

Damn, I thought as I hung up. I'd agreed to talk about it later. That meant I'd left the door open a crack. We'd have to have this same conversation all over again. One more time.

Didn't he understand? Didn't he know? A Christmas without David was too, too much to bear. There was no such thing as going home without David; the word home didn't mean anything anymore. He was my home. It was better to have no Christmas at all. Yes, better by far.

I sighed and covered my face with my pillow.

Next time, I'd make him understand. I would. I *would.*

Spending the Christmas season alone in London wouldn't be so bad. Not when I had so very much to do. It would be much easier to ignore that way.

Besides, there'd always be next Christmas.

David's picture watched me from its place on my nightstand. I touched my fingers to my lips, and then to his in the picture, a thing I'd done a thousand times, even though I hated the damn cliché. I closed my eyes tight to dam the tears inside. And before I could stop myself, I was thinking about another Christmas, a ghost of Christmas past. It was my second Christmas in England. My second with David.

We'd been in Piccadilly Arcade in the very heart of central London that day. If you don't know it, you should, even though David always called it a touristy nightmare. It's a charming place, a sort of a hybrid between an alley and a shopping mall that, at the time, I'd thought was just quintessentially English, and a perfect place to buy gifts for all the family back home in the States. I remember standing by myself, huddled against the cold, with all my bags and bundles arranged carefully at my feet, cradling an almost empty cup of hot chocolate in my mittened hands and waiting more or less patiently for David. Don't believe anyone who tells you that men shop faster than women. How could they? We have more experience.

He emerged from a shop at last, carrying a few tiny bags. His long woolen overcoat was unbuttoned and his scarf was undone, so everyone could see my handsome Englishman in the ugly Christmas sweater I'd bought him the year before. The wind mussed his sandy brown hair (which, as always, looked like it was just a week or two past due for a trim) and fogged his glasses. Dishevelment suited him. He looked absolutely delectable, if in a tweedy sort of way. I looked down at all the bags and raised my eyebrows. "Gifts for all your girlfriends?"

David nodded and smiled his crooked smile. "Yes indeed. Every . . . er, *one* of them."

We started to walk together. I carefully arranged my most persuasive smile, the one I used to practice in the mirror when I was in middle school. "Is one of them, maybe, for . . . me?"

David rolled his eyes, but he couldn't hide his own smile. "Perhaps. . . ."

"Let me see! Let me see!"

"Minx. It's not Christmas yet, is it?"

"Life is uncertain," I pointed out. "Live for the moment. Isn't that what you always say?"

"I most certainly do not. No Englishman ever says that, nor anything of the sort."

"Well. You totally should. A little spontaneity would be good for you."

"I'll schedule some in, then. Soon as I'm back to my diary."

"How about now?"

"What, and ruin Christmas? Jessie, you love Christmas. All the traditions and what not."

"I can love it just as much right now," I insisted stubbornly.

"No, you most certainly cannot. You shall wait for Christmas morning."

The smile clearly hadn't worked, so I tried puppy dog eyes. "C'mon. One present? Please? One?" I added more than one extra syllable to the middle of the please.

David laughed. "Oh, all right, you."

Bingo. Puppy dog eyes never fail. "I love you."

"You'd better," David said. God, I can still hear his voice, and that scrumptious accent. I can still smell his scent, sweet wool and sandalwood aftershave, mingled with his own salty musk. "Here."

He stopped, shifted his burdens, and offered me one gift bag, the biggest of the bunch. I looked around and—*There!*—I spotted a cafe table where I could set my bundles down. I took the bag from David and peeked inside. I grinned. The bag held a rather impressive stack of DVDs. I didn't have to shift them too much to see that they were all Christmas movies.

"David! I . . . love these! How'd you know?"

He shrugged in that awkward, adorable way of his. "Well, I didn't really, did I?" He smiled that crooked smile again. "But I do know you love Christmas, and if I didn't, well, it certainly wouldn't be because you don't remind me enough, would it? Besides, *I* do. They're my favorites. I . . . I really wanted to share them with you. But if you've seen them. . . ."

"Silly. I adore Christmas movies. I'd love to watch them with you. But we need to get *Rudolf.*"

"It's there. Look. Second from the bottom."

"I love you."

"You'd just better."

"I do!"

"Anyway. One a night until Christmas."

"One a night," I agreed. "Or maybe two. On some nights."

David beamed. "On some nights." I struggled to reassemble my many bags. "Here, let me." David reached for two of my heavier bags. "Good heavens. If these are for all your boyfriends, you must be seeing a whole football team."

I batted my eyes. "Why sir! That's all in my past."

"Hmpf."

We started walking again, darting around other shoppers and gazing into the shop windows as we passed. I caught David trying to sneak a peek into one of my bags. I would have slapped his hand, but I had all the packages, so I turned my best glare on him, the one I'd learned from Mom.

David chuckled, then turned his eyes back to the bags. "So. All this for me, then?"

"Ha! You'd like that."

"Of course I would. So who won the lottery, then?"

"Uh, yeah. About that. See, well . . . that's something I . . . uh . . . yeah. That's something I wanted to talk to you about."

David stopped. "That doesn't sound good."

Suddenly, I found I couldn't meet his gaze, so I turned my attention to the bags and pretended to sort them again. "All that about me loving Christmas?"

"Yes?"

"Well, what I really love is, uh, going *home* for Christmas."

"A little home sick, are we?"

"Sometimes. A little. Mostly at the holidays. We have all these traditions, see. Tree, midnight candlelight service, cocoa. . . . See, they all mean a lot to me, David. Christmas is about going home. Don't you think? That's pretty much what the word means to me."

"Christmas means home."

"It's sounds silly when you say it like that. But, uh, yeah. It does."

"I see."

I took a deep breath. "So. The packages and stuff. All this . . . well, most of it . . . see, it's for my family. Back home. In Alabama. In the States."

"I know where Alabama is," said David. "Well, more or less. Bottom right, er, isn't it, yes?"

"Right. I, uh . . . yeah. See, I always go home. For Christmas, I mean. It's like . . . it's a big deal for us."

"Ah." David smiled. "A big deal, then?"

I swallowed. "We all gather. Mom, dad, my brother, grandparents, aunts, uncles . . . many cousins."

"My. That *is* a big deal."

"Tree, stockings, the works." Another deep breath. *Okay. Here goes. Just say it, Jessie. Go on. Just say it.* "And, well. . . . Yeah. See, I was hoping you'd come with me."

"Of course I'll come with you."

I looked up at last. He was still smiling, and my heart melted. No, it exploded. Melted and exploded. Both of them at the same time. Like the world's biggest snowball. It was rather a mess, really. "You will?"

"I will."

"I haven't even made my pitch yet."

"You had me at the many cousins bit."

"Ha. Say that when you've met them. You're sure you won't mind? Really?"

David set his bags down on the pavement and reached down to touch my cheek. I always loved it when he did that. "Jessie, I really want to meet your family. I really do. And I most especially don't want to be apart. Not at Christmas."

"Oh?"

David reached down and found a bag, a small one. "Here. You can open another present."

"Yay!" I would have clapped my hands, but, well, the bundles. I looked around for another place to set them down again.

"Here. No, just . . . here, give." David managed to take my bags while giving me one in exchange. He knelt and set the bags on the sidewalk while I opened the bag. Inside, I found a single, lovely Christmas ornament. It looked antique, or handmade. Maybe both. It was made of blown glass, but etched with delicate patterns, like a snowflake made of crystal. It was elegant, beautiful and utterly unique. On it, someone had hand-painted words in elegant, gold-leaf script:

First Married Christmas

I gasped. "David!"

"Well, I suppose it's really for next year, isn't it?"

I looked down to find David on one knee, smiling, surrounded by all our bags and packages, holding an open ring box.

My eyes were wide as my hands went up to cover my open mouth. I could already feel the tears sliding down my cheeks. Dammit, that was not at all how I'd wanted to say yes, because I am such an ugly crier.

It took me a long time to get back to sleep. The memory wouldn't leave. It haunted me. My little room was too cold and empty without David in it. Nonetheless, I woke up early the next morning feeling tired and sad. I always wake up at the same early time, no matter how much or how little rest I manage the night before. It's like I've forgotten how to sleep late. Teenage me would be scandalized. The dark circles under my eyes had become a permanent feature, like age lines or battle scars.

A mug of coffee made me sufficiently jittery. I make a perfect cup, if I do say so; it's one of my special talents in life. David introduced me to tea, bless his heart, but given my druthers I always went back to my beloved old coffee. But despite its strong and steaming black goodness, it couldn't warm the weariness away from my bones. All the same, I made do. I buttered some toast, opened a book, found my favorite pen, and settled down to work.

More than once, thoughts of Sam's ghost flitted through the attics of my brain, like a strong wind teasing white curtains in an open window. Jason Cook, the friend who'd told me the story, had offered to take me to the pub where an Irish banker friend had told him about Sam just a few weeks ago. Honestly, I don't know where Jason finds these people. The man could make friends with a lamppost. Anyway, Jason said the Irish banker man claimed to have heard it directly from his cousin, a retired Royal Navy man. Jason had also said he could introduce me to a cabbie who'd told him another variant of the same tale several months earlier.

"I can take you to both of them," he'd said. Jason had looked away slyly before turning back to meet my gaze. He'd smiled and waggled his eyebrows. The scum. "That is, if you're interested."

I'd declined politely, of course. The first time, and then twice more. The fourth decline was less polite but no less emphatic. I couldn't spare time away from my dissertation research just because Jason Cook knew exactly how to push my buttons. And no, I most certainly did *not* need to spend more time away from the flat, no matter what he said. I had work to do.

I'm being too harsh on Jason, I suppose. He's a good friend, and he'd been a good friend to David, and I know he really does have my best interests at heart. Just like I do his when I nag him about not working on his own dissertation enough. He had a deadline, too, after all.

Jason had shrugged as he stood up to leave. "Well, if you change your mind, Mr. Colm and I'll be at The Red Lion at six on Wednesday. Just for a bite of dinner and a pint, you know. Why don't you join us, Jess? I mean, if you'd like."

"I *can't.*"

Jason had smiled again as he brushed a stray lock of hair away from his eyes. "Well, you know where to find us. If you decide you're interested in the story, that is."

Wednesday. Tonight.

But no, no, I just didn't have the time.

I opened volume after volume, checking and cross-checking variations and references, citing sources, and making notes. My cheap ballpoint pen leaked (my favorite was out of ink), staining the tips of my fingers blue, so I threw it away and found another. This one stained my fingertips black. When my hand started to cramp, I shook it and kept working. The piles of books seemed no shorter despite my best efforts. I'd only added to the post-it notes.

I opened a tin of soup for lunch and made a fresh pot of coffee. With effort, I forced myself back to work.

By two, I was sick to death of yellowed newspaper accounts, shivering priests, and pleading women in bonnets and shawls. I noticed a book Jason had left behind last time he came over to watch American TV with me. I should call him, or take it over, maybe. Or maybe I could just run it by the pub.

No. *No.* I didn't have time for that. I most absolutely did *not.*

By three, my eyes were starting to swim. By four, they were starting to burn.

I looked over at Jason's book. I thought again about taking it to him. He might need it, after all. My better instincts won out and I kept working. If Jason needed the bloody book, he could bloody well come get it.

By five, the words were blurring in front of me and I felt the beginning of a headache stirring ominously behind my temples. I rubbed them for a minute or two and tried to continue.

At half past, I gave up.

I went to make another cup of coffee but I was out of beans. I thought about switching to tea, but that made me think of David. I settled for water.

I looked back at my books. I didn't open one.

Maybe a walk would clear my head enough so that I could work into the night. God knows I wasn't getting anything done by forcing myself to stay at that little table in my kitchen. I needed to reboot my brain. I also needed food, more than a tin of soup. And coffee. I needed to replenish the coffee jar. Without really thinking about what I was doing, I put on my coat and locked the flat door. It was a good evening for a walk—chilly and of course already dark, certainly, but at least it wasn't raining. For once. The streets of London were crowded. Head down, I set a brisk pace.

I hadn't intended to go to the pub. Truly. I hadn't even brought Jason's book. In fact, I actually found myself standing in front of The Red Lion before I even realized I'd been wandering that way. I waited outside the door for a long moment, chewing my lip and wondering what to do. If I went in, I'd lose at least an hour of productive work time. Well, potentially productive time, anyway. More, since I'd still have to stop for groceries and coffee.

I did *not* have the time to spare. On the other hand, I had to admit, if reluctantly, that a break would do me good. If I took one, I might be able to work later into the night. Besides, I wouldn't have to hear about Sam's ghost just because I went in. And if it came up, well, I didn't have to get distracted by it. For one time at least, I could hear about a puzzle without having to unravel it in my mind and follow every loose end to its beginning. I could do that. Of course I could. I'd just be an hour or so. . . .

An hour I don't have, I reminded myself sternly.

To heck with it. A girl needs a bite of supper, after all. And as much as I hated to admit it, Jason had been right about one thing. I could use some actual human company. I glanced down at my watch as I considered. It was six o'clock, spot on.

David would have gone in, I reminded myself. I sighed. *Well, why not?* I decided at last. *I can enjoy a hot meal and a drink or two without getting sidetracked by a ghost story. I can do it. Of course I can.* I laughed at myself a little as I stepped inside.

Bloody hell. I totally should have known. I should have brought Jason's book.

The pub was an old place, all dark wood, beveled glass, and polished brass, almost stereotypically London. They'd already decorated it for the holidays; boughs of greenery with red ribbons and sparkling white lights draped the crowded room. I found the place homey and charming, just what the doctor ordered. David would have loved it.

I looked around and found Jason at a table in the back corner by the pub's great stone fireplace, sipping a pint of bitter. He grinned and waved me over. I returned the wave, ordered a plate of fish and chips and a pint of Old Peculier ale at the bar, and joined him.

"Hiya, Jessie," he greeted me with a sheepish smile. "You look . . . uh, well."

I smiled as I touched my hair and blushed. Since I hadn't meant to come to the pub, I hadn't bothered to fix myself up.

"I've been working," I explained. "I just went for a walk, and then, well—"

"I'm teasing," Jason said. He, of course, looked perfect in black jeans and a blue and gray wool sweater. He always looked perfect. Probably something they taught in his fraternity. David had been the same way. No wonder they'd been so close. "Of course you've been working."

"You should try it someday."

He laughed. "I just might. Someday. Hey, I'm glad you made it, pal. Jeez, it's good to hear a real live American accent. God, I'll buy you a pint and kiss you if you'll talk to me about football. Real football, I mean. Not soccer."

"I'll see what I can do. If you'll talk to *me* about what's happening on *This Is Us* this season." I meant that. American TV kept me sane this far from home.

Jason shrugged.

"Let me guess. You don't watch *This Is Us*, do you?"

Jason shrugged again.

"You don't even care what's happening on *This Is Us*, do you?"

"If you can somehow work the phrase 'rat's ass' in there, you'll have it."

"Snooty pretentious anti-television bias?"

Jason grinned. "I don't have any more spare time than you do, Jessie ol' pal. I just choose to spend my time out in the world meeting real people instead of watching TV that I'll be able to see on streaming pretty much from now on when I get back home."

"So how does American football get you out among the throng?"

"That's different. Besides, I can work while I watch."

"Philistine," I accused. "Football it is."

"American style. No bloody soccer. That doesn't count. No real sport has spots on the ball. That's not a sport. It's . . . it's an *activity*."

"I love that you think I'll know the difference. But sure. So. Who's your favorite batter?"

He looked at me with wide eyes and gaping mouth. I winked, but he scowled anyway. It did not deter him. I settled back. For the moment at least, talking about football, American, not soccer, beat the heck out of researching pleading ghosts and vanishing hitchhikers. It would pass the time pleasantly enough, but it wouldn't distract me from my work. That was the idea, anyway. But Jason's banker friend, a smartly dressed Irish man called Colm Jameson, arrived just then and we ordered another round. Colm's thinning gray hair was neatly combed and he wore a tie patterned with Christmas holly. Despite the fact that business hours were over, he hadn't loosened his perfect Windsor knot.

We chatted pleasantly. Neither of them even mentioned Sam's ghost. That just infuriated me. You'd think they'd at least talk about poor Sam just to satisfy my curiosity and get it over with. But no. They passed the time arguing about the respective merits of British versus American sports. They both made many points, of which I followed a total of exactly zero.

What were they waiting for? Surely Jason remembered why he'd invited me in the first place. For Heaven's sake, he wasn't *that* big a sports buff. I'd known him since high school; he never had been. Although come to think of it, he and David used to argue about it all the time. I'd learned to tune them both out. That's when I realized what Jason was doing. He wanted me to bring up Sam's ghost so that I couldn't blame him later. *Ha.* I'd show him. I wouldn't bring up Sam at all. I'd simply enjoy the conversation and head back to my tiny flat and my books. With coffee. No distractions, not for this girl. I needed to be working.

And then I'd find a way to blame him anyway.

My willpower didn't last much longer, though. After about twenty minutes of debate over which sport was real football, I caved. I took a long sip and licked the creamy foam away from my lips. Then, despite my best intentions, I found myself casually but artfully turning the conversation to Colm's cousin, and to Sam's ghost.

To his credit, Jason made an effort to hide his smug little smile. I made a point of studiously ignoring him just the same.

3

The Disappearing Sailor

e ordered a round of Irish coffees. Colm blew into his mug and look a long sip, slurping carefully to avoid burning his lips and tongue. Then he leaned back in his chair and, in the dancing, red-gold light of the crackling fire, began his story.

"It was Christmas Eve," he began. He rubbed his chin for a moment, as though remembering, even though this was clearly a tale he told often. "This would be two years ago, the year it snowed. A white Christmas, sure, and right here in London. Do you remember that? Or wait, that'd be before you came over, wouldn't it?"

"I missed the famous London White Christmas," I acknowledged.

"One of the great disappointments of my life," said Jason. "I thought it *always* snowed in London at Christmas."

"You've been reading too much Dickens," I said, waggling a finger at him.

"Ah," Colm said with a broad wink. "But it did snow back in Mister Dickens' day, didn't it? Everyone knows that. I think the Gulf Stream must've worked differently for those few decades, as it were. Just for the benefit of Mister Scrooge and his ilk."

We all chuckled.

"I knew it," Jason declared with a satisfied nod.

"You were saying?" I prompted Colm.

"Right," said Colm. "Where was I, then?"

"Christmas Eve," I reminded him.

"Just so, just so," said Colm. "Now, then. This was that same Christmas when we had the snow, wasn't it? That night, my cousin Mickey Smythe had been at a little pub down by the old docks along the Thames, a little place called The Admiral's Men. It's a favorite of his, and he goes there every year on Christmas Eve to raise a pint or two with his old lads from the Navy. It's a sort of tradition of his, y'see. Although this was a sad night for them, sure. One of their mates had just passed on, rest his soul. It hit Mickey pretty hard, didn't it? Ah, but they all raised a pint to his memory, sure. And another one after that. Just to show their proper respect and all."

So he'd been drinking, I thought. *Whatever else happens in this story, I'll have to keep that in mind.*

"Did you hear this from your cousin directly?" I asked him.

"Oh, no, no," Colm admitted. "Old Mickey, see, he told it to his mum, who told it to her sister. That'd be my own mum, if you follow me. She told it to my brother Stephen, sure, and didn't he tell it straight to me himself?"

"I see," I said with a nod. *Not exactly an original source, but he's actually attributed it to someone specific, not some vague friend of a friend.* That was new in my experience. "So, what happened?"

"It happened just like this," said Colm. "Mickey and his mates finished their second pints and wished one another a happiest of holidays, poured one out for their fallen mate, rest his soul, and promised to meet again the next year, right back there at The Admiral's Men, same as always. Mickey was the first to leave. He had to get home to gather his own family and get them all to Mum's house in time to get all the wee ones to bed before Father Christmas came, didn't he?"

Jason and I smiled and nodded. Colm took another sip and continued.

"Now then. As soon as old Mick left the pub, well, didn't the snow pick up again? It got so bad that he couldn't see more than ten yards in front of him, sure as I'm born. But Mick, he knew that people were a-waiting for him back home, sure, so he made his way right on anyway. He brushed the snow off his windshield, started his car, and drove on all slow and careful like, seein' as how the roads were so slick and dangerous.

"Now then, Mickey hadn't driven a wink away from the docks, when he saw a man, sure, standing right in the middle of the road and trying to flag him down. As bad as the snow was, Mick nearly ran the poor bloke down before he even saw him. But God and his angels were looking out for him that Christmas Eve night and Mick stopped in time, if just barely. Mick probably would have just started on again and driven on his way, but he happened to notice that the chap was wearin' a Royal Navy uniform. Well, Mick couldn't very well leave a fellow sailor in need out there in the storm, could he?"

"Not a bit of it," Jason agreed with a grin.

"No indeed," said Colm. "Especially not on Christmas Eve. Besides, the man reminded Mick of this old mate, the man who'd just died, naturally enough. So he opened his window and called out to the chap: 'You there! Is there trouble, then?'

"'Praise God!' said the young man. 'I didn't think anybody'd ever stop! Can you give me a lift, then? Please, mate, I'm desperate—'

"Old Mick now, he frowned, rememberin' that the family would be home and waitin' for him. But like I said, he couldn't just leave a Navy man, could he? Of course not. Not when the weather was so bad. 'Hop in,' said Mickey. 'But be quick about it, eh? The family's expecting me.'

"Well now, that sailor grinned just as big as he could as he ran around to the passenger side and climbed in, fast as you please. 'Thanks a lot, mate!' said the man. 'You don't know what this means to me! I promised my girl

I'd be home for Christmas, and I was scared to death I wouldn't make it!'

"'Don't you worry about it, then, friend,' said Mickey. 'I'll just hurry on and get us both home before the first carol's half sung, sure.'

"The man gave Mick an address up in Hampstead. Now Mick and his family live way over in Greenwich, so that was quite a drive. But Mick knew that the best way to hurry a long drive was to get started, so he did just that. Just as he did, the young sailor offered Mick his hand to shake. 'The name's Sam Prescott,' said the man. Mickey took the man's hand and introduced himself in turn. Sam's grip was strong but cold. Mickey shivered a bit, he did.

"As they drove through the bitter and snowy night, Sam told Mick a little bit about himself. Seems the lad had married himself an American girl called Emily just before he'd shipped out. They hadn't even had themselves a proper honeymoon, no indeed. But they'd be together for the holy day. The lad had promised! Mick, now, he smiled. He aimed to see that boy keep his promise to his poor Emily. The wife would understand. Sure, she'd have his hide if he did anything else but help the poor boy, she would!

"Given the dark and the situation, you can understand why Mick didn't notice that Sam's Royal blues were a little . . . well, old fashioned, let's say.

"As they drove, Sam looked out at the city with eyes as wide as good Sunday dinner plates. Mick couldn't help chuckling just a little bit. 'Haven't been to the city much then, have you?'

"'Not too much, mate,' the boy admitted with a shrug. 'I'm a north-country man. London, now . . . it always seems so different . . . even bigger and more crowded than I remember.'

"'Well, that's mostly the snow,' said Mick. 'And it'll probably seem like that next time, too, God willing. I don't expect that pretty Yank girl of yours'll be letting you out of the house too much to explore, will she?' Mickey winked. Poor Sam blushed and looked away. Mickey grinned. 'Well, I'm sure she'll have a big, steaming-hot Christmas dinner just waiting for you, pretty as you please and with all the trimmings, eh?'

"'I don't know about that,' said Sam, 'what with the rationing and all. But whatever she has there, it'll be a feast to me. Look out!'

"Mickey had to turn the wheel quickly, because a skidding black cab narrowly missed them. That put poor Mick in a skid, too, but thankfully he merely slid into the curb. No one was hurt. 'Jesus, Mary, and Joseph!' exclaimed Mick. 'Are you all right, Sam?'

"'Just a bit shaken,' said Sam. 'Look, there's the turn up there, mate. D'you see?'

"Mick made the turn, and the one after that. Sam's directions took them deep into the twisting, maze-like

45

streets of Hampstead. Have you two been up to that part of London?"

"I haven't," I admitted.

"I have a time or two," Jason said as he finished the last of his Irish coffee. "I got myself lost every single time. I swear, the map and the streets around the tube station just don't seem to match up, do they?"

Colm nodded. "That's easy enough to do, Jason my friend. Only a local-born or a cabbie can find his way around thereabouts, and that's a fact. Mick's car slid a little, but he made the final turn the boy pointed out. Then, just a block or two further, he slid to a stop right where the lad told him, in front of one of those plain detached brick flat buildings that are going up everywhere in the workin' neighborhoods. 'Here you are, boyo, sure as you please. Happy Christmas to you, sir, and to your sweet American girl, too.'

"'But this can't be right!' cried the boy.

"'Eh? What's that then?'

"'This isn't it! This isn't our building,' said Sam.

"'Well, not to worry,' said Mick. 'We must have missed a turn. Lord knows that's easy enough to do up here, especially in the snow. Let's back around and try again, shall we?'

"They did just that, Mickey and this fellow Sam, and sure enough, they wound up right back at that very same place again. Poor Sam's confusion was getting close to panic, but my cousin, he kept a level head. They circled around more slowly, this time checking the surrounding streets and alleys, just in case the lad had managed to get things turned around in his head. Now and then, things would look familiar to the boy, but more often they didn't. Each time, they wound up back at that same spot—that very same address Sam had given old Mick right at the start.

"And let me tell you this, my young friends. It was getting pretty close to late by that point, you can be sure. Mick had to be getting home. But he hadn't the heart to just abandon the boy, did he? 'I promised her,' said Sam. His cheeks were wet with tears. 'I promised her I'd be home for Christmas. . . .'

"'There now,' said Mick. 'No need to worry, Sam. We'll get you there. Maybe we just need to ask the way of someone here abouts.' They twisted through the streets once again, and once again they came back to that same building. By now, Sam was close to the point of hysteria. Mick now, he didn't say a word. He slid his car to a stop on the slick street and, without even bothering to turn off the motor, climbed out. He thought to knock someone up and see what's what, or perhaps get a spot of directions. Maybe there's another street with the same name close by. You never know what they'll do up in Hampstead, do you?"

"I do not," Jason admitted.

Colm looked us both in the eye, one by one, and then lowered his deep voice almost to a whisper before he continued.

"The snow picked up something fierce as he climbed that slippery walkway towards the door. Mick was thinking that even if the people there couldn't point the way, well, at least they'd let him use the telephone, wouldn't they? It was Christmas Eve, after all. And even if Sam couldn't call his girl, well, at least Mick would be able to call the family and let 'em know where he was and what he was about. Maybe he could take Sam home with him and start over again in the morning light. Sam would protest, of course, but they couldn't very well drive around lost all night, could they?

"Mick knocked on the door. Just a moment or two later, a man opened it. 'Ho there,' said Mick. 'Sorry to disturb you so late, and on Christmas Eve no less. . . .'

"The man there shook his head and smiled. 'No worries, sir,' said he. 'I've been waiting up.'

"'Well then,' said Mick, 'I'm hoping you might help me with some directions, or maybe let me use your telephone—'

"The man laughed and shook his head. 'You've brought Sam, haven't you? The Navy man?'

"Mick was astonished. 'I have for a fact! Have we found the right place after all?'

"The man there just shook his head and laughed again. 'I'm sure I can't help you,' the bloke said. 'But I've

lived right here for seven years now, and somebody stops 'round every Christmas Eve about this time, trying to get a sailor named Sam home to his bride for Christmas. That's how I know to wait up, y'see. I could just about set my watch, I could.'

"'But that can't be!' cried poor Mick.

"'Oh, it's the truth, and didn't the lady who owns place didn't tell me the same thing used to happen to her when she lived here?'

"Mick's jaw nearly hit the doorstep. The man gave him a sympathetic smile and a friendly slap on the arm. 'Why don't you get on home then? You'll find that your car's empty now, I fancy.'"

Colm set his empty mug down on the wooden table as he finished. His eyes narrowed as he regarded Jason and me. "Old Mick made his way back to the car and sure enough, wasn't it just as empty as a beggar's bank-book? Sam was gone, vanished like the night at dawn.

"And do you want to know what's more, then? Mick circled around twice, just to be sure. The only tracks in the snow leading away from that car were his own.

"And that, my friends, is the Gospel truth, every word, sure as I'm born."

As we left the pub together a bit later, Jason looked down at me and smiled, just a little smugly. "Not a bad yarn, eh?"

I shrugged, not wanting to admit I was intrigued. "Pretty much what you told me," I replied. "Colm tells it well, though. He should be a professional. But it's still just a variation on the Vanishing Hitchhiker motif." The wind had picked up and the London night was chillier. I wished I'd brought a heavier coat, not to mention my scarf and gloves.

"With some interesting differences, don't you think?"

I shrugged again. "Maybe. Potentially."

"And not a vague friend of a friend," Jason prodded, "but an actual named source. One you just might be able to interview. . . ."

"Humbug," I said. "That Mick probably just needed an excuse to tell his family. He was probably down at that pub all night drinking with his pals."

Jason laughed. "That's my pal Jess. Still though, an original source. And wait till you hear the cabbie's version."

"Have Mick and your cabbie friend compared notes?"

Jason's grin widened. "As God is my witness, they've never met."

"So what's their connection?"

"I've checked and double checked," said Jason. "There's nothing. Nothing at all."

"There must be," I said. *You just haven't looked hard enough.*

"There's absolutely no connection between them. None at all."

There is *a connection, Jason. There's you.* I kept that thought to myself.

"Interested yet?"

Yes, I thought.

"No, no, *no,*" I admonished him. "Jason, I just don't have time! It's interesting, of course it is. But I have a dissertation, okay?"

"I know, I know. You promised David."

"I did. I promised myself, too."

Jason laughed again, holding up his hands in surrender. "Okay, okay. I won't bring it up again. I promise. But it *does* seem worth investigating, doesn't it?"

"Maybe later. When I'm finished. Or at least when I get my head above water again. God, you should see how much I have to finish before I go off to the Paris libraries next week. Speaking of which, why don't you come with me? There's probably stuff there you can use, too."

He gave me a lopsided grin. "Well, I'm not usually the type to say no to a trip to romantic Paris with a beautiful woman. . . ."

"It's a work trip, Romeo," I scolded him. "Besides, don't you have a girlfriend?"

"Not this week."

"Carrie?"

"Last week. Single now."

"Good. You can help me work."

"You make it sound so appealing," he returned dryly. "But even though it means missing a trip to Disneyland Paris—"

"No, it doesn't. Even if we had the time, we would *not* be spending it at Disneyland."

He smirked. "Whatever you say. But I can't, Jess. You know that."

I stopped. "Why not?"

He quirked his head as he turned back and regarded me, looking genuinely puzzled. "What do you mean, why not?"

I lifted an eyebrow. "What's unclear?"

"It's Christmas, Jessie. I'm going home."

"Right. Of course you are."

"Even I have too much to do if I'm going to finish everything I have to before my flight. Kidding aside, I do have a ton of work. I can't spare the time for Paris, I'm afraid. Much as I'd like to."

I looked away. Good, we were close to my block. I could be working again soon. "So how do you find the time for that?"

"Find the time? It's *Christmas*, Jessie. Time for going home."

"Like Sam's ghost?" I teased him.

"Exactly," Jason agreed with a nod.

4

The Parisian Puzzle

y French was much rustier than I'd realized. All the same, I'd managed to board the right train, find my way to the affordable hotel I'd booked, order a meal, and not perpetuate too many stereotypes about the ugly American. David would have been proud. I'd even managed to find my way to the proper library without assistance, although I'd had to break down and ask the reference librarian for help locating the specific volumes I required.

I made it a productive day. I worked through supper, pausing only to buy a bitter coffee from a vending machine (it tasted positively English; I'd hoped for better from the French). When a voice calling over the loudspeaker announced closing time—I think that's what he said, anyway—I actually allowed myself a brief smile of pride as I looked back over what I'd accomplished. I didn't have checkout privileges, of course, but the librarians were kind enough to keep the volumes behind the desk for me, complete with my post-it note bookmarks, so they'd be there waiting for me in the morning.

I thought briefly about exploring the city and enjoying a little Parisian nightlife, but I thought better of it. I'd be fresher in the morning if I got plenty of sleep. After all, I'd need an early start and a fresh mind if I expected to get enough done with my limited time in Paris. And to be honest, I couldn't face the thought of wandering through romantic Paris without David. I did treat myself to a nice glass of red wine with dinner, though.

I bought a chocolate almond croissant and an espresso the next morning, finished them, and was there waiting when the library opened. I stayed focused all the way through early afternoon, even though my still-rusty French made the reading an arduous process. My mind started to wander a bit around two, though. I was slightly ahead of schedule, so I decided to indulge in a little lunch. I found a nearby café with patio seating and chose a little table for one. While I waited, I watched a couple on the sidewalk, dancing slowly to the lovely sound of cello music played by a nearby busker. Only in Paris. I sighed.

I ate alone, missing David so much I ached.

David wanted us to take dancing lessons.

I looked back at him with narrowed eyes. I had absolutely no idea whether or not he was serious, which I confess was a not-uncommon occurrence. "Dancing lessons?"

He nodded, grinning. "Dancing lessons."

"Might I ask . . . what brought this on?"

"What do you mean?"

"Why, exactly, do you want dance classes?"

"Why?"

"Why."

"Why, your family Christmas celebration, of course!"

"You want to dance. At my mom and dad's house. At Christmas."

"Sure," said David. "And why not, eh? Isn't that what you all do down there?" He actually said you all. In all the time I'd known him, David had never once mastered a proper *y'all*. "A right proper Southern holiday hoedown?"

"We most certainly do not!"

"Your family doesn't have a Christmas hoedown?"

"I don't think anybody does that."

"Not in Alabama?"

"Not anywhere. I'm pretty sure that's not a thing."

He looked at me, his expression a mixture of disappointment and stunned bewilderment. He couldn't hold that look for long, and before I'd thought of a single thing to say, I caught him trying to stifle a grin that was twitching at the edge of his lip.

I rolled my eyes. "Oh . . . you!" I'll admit it wasn't one of my snappier comebacks.

"I was serious about the dance lessons," David added after I'd punched him in the shoulder.

I pulled the narrowed eye look out again and slid it back on, ready to punch his shoulder again if need be.

"Really!" he insisted.

"Again with the, uh, why, exactly?"

"Why?"

"Why," I confirmed.

He laughed softly. "Silly girl. For our wedding, of course. I want to give you the fairy tale first dance you've always dreamed of."

I returned his grin. "I'm not sure that's something I've ever dreamed of. Or even thought of, really."

"Well, one of us has, anyway. C'mon, Jess." He smiled. His smile was his equivalent of my puppy dog eyes. "It'll be fun. And romantic. What do you say?"

I laughed and nodded. David beamed.

And so, a couple of days later, we crossed the Thames and followed some less-than-perfect directions to a dance studio on Clapham High Street, which was about as London sounding a name as one can imagine.

Inside, a prim woman with thin lips welcomed us. She had a lean, strong build beneath her simple black sweater and skirt, and I found it easy to imagine her having had a career on the stage in her younger days.

"Right, then," she said after she'd introduced herself. "Lessons, is it? And for the both of you, yes?"

"For our wedding," I said proudly.

"Excellent! And what sort of dance, then?" She winked. "Tango? A rose for the gentleman's teeth?"

"That sounds hard," said David. "We only have a few months."

"Ballroom then?" She winked again. "Disco?"

David and I answered at the same time. "Ballroom," I said.

"Disco," said David.

We looked at each for a second, blinking.

I turned back to the woman. "Disco," I said firmly, nodding.

"Wow," said David. "I thought that was going to require considerably more discussion."

"My love, you have no idea what I'd give to see you attempting disco at our wedding."

"Right then," the woman with the thin lips said. "How's next Wednesday to start, then? Half past six in the evening?"

"Perfect," I said. David nodded, grinning like a child.

"It's all settled, then," the woman said.

As we left, I stole a quick glance at the woman's calendar where she'd made her notes. The Wednesday class she'd signed us up for was Ballroom for Beginners.

I made sure David didn't see the smile I hid behind my hand.

We started the very next Wednesday, at half past six in the evening. Our first class went . . . well, better than I'd expected, although the next morning I had so many bruises on the tops of my feet that I couldn't wear real shoes for two whole days. The one after that was better; the bruises faded after a day or so. After six classes, David was getting much closer to what one might charitably call semi-graceful. He almost never stepped on my feet at all. Not more than once or twice, anyway.

I finished my lonely meal and paid the bill. The couple was still dancing as I left. I dropped a couple of Euros in the cellist's case.

When I returned to the library some thirty minutes later, I found it a bit difficult to find my concentration again. I kept finding little excuses to keep from starting—organizing my notes, stacking the books, sharpening my pencils. At last I forced myself to open the next book in my pile, *Histoires et Légendes de Fantôme Européennes du Vingtième Siècle,* a collection of 20th Century European ghost legends. But for once, I didn't go straight to the index. Instead, I flipped through it idly, studying the rather garish illustrations, reading a paragraph here, skimming a page there.

And then my heart stopped.

One of the tales, one recorded here in Paris in the late 1960s, was a variation on the good old Vanishing Hitchhiker motif. It was about a British Naval sailor. A young man named Sam Prescott.

I shook my head. It couldn't be. It *couldn't!*

But there it was, in plain black and white. I had to read it three times to be sure I hadn't somehow gotten it wrong. My French wasn't *that* bad. The tale was clearly a variation on the very one Colm had told Jason and me at The Red Lion Pub back in London. Every detail was the same, literally every single one, save for the location and date.

On Christmas Eve, a woman stopped to pick up a hitchhiker, a young British sailor named Sam Prescott. Sam was desperate to make it to London because he'd promised his pretty bride, an American woman, that he'd be home for Christmas. The account even confirmed the American woman's name: Emily.

According to the account, Sam had been hitchhiking across Europe, desperate to make it to London. The driver, who'd been returning from a dear friend's funeral, brought him as far as Paris. When she stopped just before midnight, he'd disappeared. She'd only looked away for a moment, but he'd vanished without a trace. Only the cold lingered.

Every important detail matched. Almost too precisely.

I chewed my lower lip for a moment. I didn't have time for this kind of distraction, but my mind couldn't let go of the puzzle. I might not have the Ph.D. hanging on my wall yet, but I was a trained cultural anthropologist—and

I'd stumbled upon an anomaly I couldn't explain. Sam's variation was common enough on the surface, but truly, it seemed to just defy the ways urban legends were supposed to spread.

I tried to talk myself out of chasing this thing. I really did. I didn't have the time for a distraction. I hadn't even organized my post-its. But I knew I'd never be able to let go of the riddle until I'd solved it. Sighing rather too loudly for a library, I reached for the stack of books I'd already worked through, this time looking for mentions of Sam rather than Pleading Ghost variations.

By the time the library closed that evening, I'd exhausted the resources there. I'd found at least twelve specific references, and possibly as many as forty that might reasonably be considered "folk process" variations on Sam's story—meaning that a friend of a friend had passed the account along to the point where the details had become somewhat muddled by the time they were recorded.

I also found seven that seemed to be at most two reports removed from an original source. In any case, the details were close enough to be significant—the name Sam Prescott, British Navy, American wife in London, home for Christmas. In more than a few, the driver had been returning from a funeral or a wake, or something of the sort. They'd each lost someone close to them, an unusual variation in the Vanishing Hitchhiker genre. The oldest dated from the late forties, the most recent from the late seventies or early eighties.

Sam always appeared on December 24, Christmas Eve. The only significant detail that changed was the starting location and the year. It was a stretch, but Sam's story seemed to have slowly, year to year, moved across Western Europe until he arrived in Paris in the fifties. He seemed to reappear there in account after account through the eighties, although a tabloid newspaper account reported a story that was also close enough to be significant (the details matched, but they didn't mention the name Prescott) in 1993.

So Sam's ghost flitted about Paris once a year until the early 1990s, and then he disappeared. The Vanishing Hitchhiker.

But I knew where he'd gone. He'd gone to London.

Hmmm. The early '90s. Wait. Isn't that when the Chunnel opened? Maybe Sam finally managed to hitchhike under the English Channel!

I laughed at my own unspoken joke, but then I frowned. It didn't make sense. I was right—Sam's story defied the models for how urban legends were supposed to spread. My pulse quickened a bit as I considered the possibilities. If I could find enough corroborating sources, I might have reason to challenge some of the prevailing theories of contemporary mythology. This was the kind of opportunity a cultural anthropologist dreamed of.

The problem was, I didn't have time to follow it up. I had a dissertation to finish. I'd promised David. One of us, at least, should keep a bloody promise.

David and I met at a party at the university. We happened to be in line together at the bar, and we started chatting, as one does. He liked my dress; I liked his suit. He had just finished his studies; I'd just come over to begin my graduate work. Once we had our drinks, we kept right on talking. David was on an alumni advisory board, which, I learned, mostly involved hobnobbing and fundraising. He was supposed to be doing both at the party, but instead, he spent most of his time with me. When he asked me to get a drink with him afterward, I accepted. He looked so dashing in that suit!

We agreed to meet for another drink over the weekend, and we met again for lunch the very next day. We met twice the next week, and twice more over the weekend. In all that time, we never once ran out of things to talk about. That might be the surest way to know one is falling in love. That, and the first kiss, of course. We'd been seeing each other for nearly three weeks when David broached the subject. We'd enjoyed a lovely dinner Italian dinner—not the best choice when one is expecting a first kiss, but I have a gift for slipping myself breath mints, and (thank heaven!) David had it too. David walked me back to my flat and I chewed my lip while I tried to think of a casual way to invite him in.

"Jessie," David said as we stood awkwardly at my front door, "I would very much like to kiss you now."

"Oh, think dinner and a few glasses of wine entitle you to a kiss, do you?"

"What? Oh, heavens. No! Jessie—!"

I laughed. "David, I'm joking."

"Ah. Well. Thank heaven. One can't be too careful, you know. I say, the university has a policy, you know—"

I held a finger to his lips. "David. This would be the time to stop talking and kiss me. Otherwise, I am going to kiss you first, and I didn't even buy you an appetizer."

He did. It was a good first kiss indeed.

I invited him in. We had our second kiss on that little sofa in my flat, and our third kiss as well. We kissed a lot that night.

Another month passed before David told me he loved me. I actually cried a little.

"I love you, too," I said. "I truly, truly do. I only wish I'd been the one to say it first." Because in that moment I knew that saying I love you first is the bravest thing one can do in the whole world.

That night, we stayed up late, sitting on my little sofa and talking. Mostly talking. We kissed a lot, too. We told each other about our hopes, our dreams, our families . . . all the usual things one talks about after saying I love you for the first time. David's parents were both academics, it turned out, professors at Oxford. In fact, his mother had been an anthropologist before she retired.

"I always thought I'd follow in their footsteps," David told me. His smile was a sad one. "I thought I'd be the next scholar in the family. Funny, isn't it?"

I rested my head on his shoulder. "Why didn't you?"

"I found out I had a knack for the numbers and finance. I know that sounds rather boring, but, well, I . . . I rather like it, actually. There's poetry in the numbers, if one knows how to look. And while the senior partners may be slave drivers, well, I found a firm that happens to think the business of business isn't just business. It's making the world a better place. I rather like that, too."

"That must be nice. Sometimes, I think I'm just wasting my time. Like, does the world even really need another cultural anthropologist? I mean, I'm sure not going to make the world a better place."

"Knowledge always makes the world better. Don't you think? How can we improve if we don't bother to understand ourselves?"

I smiled. "I like that thought."

"Me, too. Sometimes . . . sometimes I wish I'd stayed in academia. Continued the old family tradition, as it were."

"Family traditions are good."

"So they are."

"Is that why you're on the alumni advisory board? So you can still keep one foot in the good ol' uni?"

David blinked. "I hadn't thought of that. Why, I do believe you're right!"

"Ha! And I can't get through fast enough."

"Don't say that, Jessie! How can you do the work you do if you don't love it?"

"I do love it. I truly, truly do. Well, usually."

"Maybe you can be the academic for both of us. How about that, eh? You can be the one to keep the tradition alive. How about that, eh?"

I didn't answer. I kissed him instead, the most loving and passionate kiss I knew how to give, one I knew would curl his toes. You see, I liked that idea, the idea of doing something for both of us, I liked the idea of us being partners, and I liked the idea of being a part of his tradition. Mostly, I loved that he seemed to be in this for the long haul. I think that was the exact moment I realized that I was, too.

The end of the semester came, and exams were brutal. The papers that I'd fallen behind on were worse still. That was a time when I most certainly did not love what I was doing. During that time, I was up way past midnight one night when the frustration rose in me like a storm. A dam inside me burst, and all of a sudden I wanted to sweep all the papers and coffee mugs right off my table. I wanted to break things and throw other things. I wanted to close my eyes and scream until my throat was raw. With all sincerity, I was ready to open the windows and throw my books as far as I could.

It was David who held me, and kissed me, and talked me off the (mostly) proverbial ledge.

"You're going to be the academic for both of us, aren't you?"

"Maybe not."

"Yes you are."

"I mean, what the hell, right? I can wait tables without a stupid sheepskin on the wall as well as I could with one. Why am I even putting myself though all this?"

"Because you love it. Because it's your life's work. Isn't it?"

When I didn't answer, he wrapped his arms around my waist and held me close, my back against his chest. He kissed the top of my head and I felt some of the tension melting away from my body.

"You can do this, Jessie. My love. You're just having a bad day." That much was true, even if I wasn't ready to admit it. Still, I wasn't quite ready to climb out of my self-pity bath. "You can do this. You will. You're the toughest person I know."

"Then you need to meet more people."

He kissed my head again. "I've already met the best one. You're the toughest, and the smartest, too. Which is quite saying something indeed, because I know my parents."

I closed my eyes. "I don't know if I can do this, David."

"Of course you can. For both of us. You'll finish. You'll be Doctor Jessie Malone."

"If you say so."

"No. You say so. Seriously. I want you to say it. Right now. Tell me you're going to finish.

I sighed. David kissed me on the top of the head again.

"Jessie? Say it."

"I'm going to finish."

"That's my girl. Tell me you're going to do it for both of us."

"I'm going to do it for both of us."

"Now promise me. Promise me, because I know you'll always keep your promises to me. Promises to the one you love are sacred."

Despite the storm and the frustration and the wanting to throw or break things and all that, I smiled. "I can do it. I will do it. I promise."

He kissed the top of my head one more time. I put my hands on his. Someone who loves you on a bad day really loves you.

David helped me through that exam period, and all the exam periods and paper deadlines that followed. With his help, I got through them all. Every time the light of my confidence so much as flickered, David was there to bring me coffee, or chocolate, or wine, or sometimes all of them at once.

Every time, he said the same thing. "You'll be the scholar for both of us, won't you?"

"I will."

"You'll be Doctor Jessie Malone."

"I promise."

That's what got me through, that promise. Even after he was gone, that's how I held myself together. That's how I avoided getting lost in the grief. That's how I kept going. That's how I got out of bed in the morning. Because I'd promised David, and a promise to the one I love is sacred.

The loudspeaker voice gave the final closing announcement. Spending the night in the library hardly sounded like an unappealing prospect to me, but I doubted the French authorities would share my enthusiasm. Reluctantly, I returned my materials to their places and left.

I didn't go back to my hotel. Instead, I bundled up and went for a walk through the crystal-clear cold Parisian night. Frosty breaths punctuated my steps like puffs from a steam locomotive, and I picked up my pace, hugging myself against the cold and missing David with fresh and cruel acuity.

They say the City of Lights is the most beautiful city in the world, and, while my travel experience is admittedly limited, they'll get no argument from me. That night, my lonely path carried me along and across the river and toward the Latin Quarter. But I can honestly say I didn't see a single thing. Paris is not a city to experience alone. More, Sam's ghost haunted my thoughts. Try as I might, I couldn't let the puzzle go. I plainly didn't have time for a distraction. How could I *possibly* waste time investigating the tale and its aberrant variations?

How could I not?

5

The German Apparition

hen I finally made it back to my hotel room, I made a phone call. I didn't even bother to calculate the time difference between Paris and London; I simply couldn't stand to make myself wait. I needed advice, I'd decided, and I just couldn't make myself wait for it. I heard distant ringing, those quaint European tones, and then, exactly four heartbeats later, Dr. Scheuer, my university program advisor, answered. Dr. Scheuer was the professor who'd recommended me for the Reilly Foundation fellowship that allowed me to work on my dissertation in England.

"Hello?" *She doesn't sound sleepy. Thank God, maybe I didn't wake her.*

"Hi, Dr. Scheuer," I said. "It's me, Jessie Malone."

"Jessie! My goodness. How's Paris?"

"Actually, I'm kind of thinking of maybe leaving for Germany now." And then, without preamble, I told her what I'd learned about Sam's ghost, starting with Jason and Colm and ending with the tantalizing references I'd discovered here in France.

"My!" Dr. Scheuer said when I'd finished. "That *is* intriguing! Would you email your notes over when you happen to have a free moment? I'd absolutely love to have a look."

"I will," I promised. "But you see my dilemma."

"No," she replied, sounding genuinely puzzled. "I'm not sure I do."

"Huh?" I said, demonstrating my brilliance once again to my advisor.

"I don't see your dilemma," Dr. Scheuer said patiently. "You've decided to work with urban legends to see if they might somehow be a form of modern mythology, right?"

Not sure where she was heading, I hesitated just a brief second before answering. "Right."

"You want to see what role these stories play in a modern society hungry for meaning, to see if they're somehow a symptom of missing archetypal patterns in a culture that lacks tradition and ritual. Right so far?"

"Check."

"And here you've found what seems like a cultural anthropologist's dream. Yes? A chance to very possibly trace a recurring urban legend back to a primary source!"

I chewed my lip before answering. My ear was getting a little numb from the pressure of the earpiece, so I shifted the phone to my other hand. "Right at the same time I have dissertation work due," I said at last. "Just my luck."

"Let me ask you this," she said. "Why do you want to earn your Ph.D.?"

"I don't understand."

"I think you do."

"Uh, because I've been working my butt off your years now? Because I need to graduate and get a job?"

"Jessie."

"And … and because I promised David," I said weakly. "I . . . I promised him. I promised I'd finish." It took all the effort I could muster not to cry. I wasn't going to cry, not with the professor on the line. "We both made promises. To each other, I mean. I guess I'm the only one who can keep one of them, aren't I?"

"David. You think you're doing this for David."

"Well? Why not? I haven't even let myself process the grief properly, because I've pushing to get this dissertation finished!"

"Wait. You haven't let yourself grieve because of a *dissertation?*"

"Deadlines. You know."

"That sounds like an excuse. And not a very healthy one." I didn't answer. I didn't want to lie, not to either of us. "You have to grieve, Jessie. All of it, all the stages. You can't let go until you grieve."

"Well who says I want to let go, then? Besides, if . . . if I do that, I don't know if I'll ever be able to stop. And then I'll *never* finish, will I? Well?"

"Oh, Jessie! You poor, poor dear. But let me ask my original question another way. Why did David want you to promise him? Why did he want you to finish so badly?"

"We both wanted to."

"But *why*, Jessie?"

"I . . . I don't understand."

"It's a simple question, Jessie."

That didn't help me answer it. I heard Dr. Scheuer breathing on the other end for a long moment, and once again I marveled at the miracle of instant communications with someone in another country, even one just across a narrow body of water. Funny how the mind wanders when one doesn't know what to say.

"I'll put it yet another way," she said after a few uncomfortable minutes. "What is it you're after? What were you both after? Knowledge? Learning? Or a sheepskin on your wall?"

"That, uh, knowledge and learning thing," I said without hesitation. "We both . . . we both loved that. It's part of what made us close. And . . . and I was to do it for both of us."

"Right. So, what would David do?"

I chuckled in spite of myself. "He'd run this thing down like a dog after a squirrel. Or some very proper

English variation of that saying. Foxes, I guess. Anyway. He'd go for the knowledge."

"That's my girl. Now, then. Here it is. *This* is what you're looking for, Jess. This is the opportunity you've been working so hard for, isn't it? It's what David was cheering you on for, wasn't it? That's why you were so perfect for each other. And let me tell you something else. As your advisor, of course. Opportunities like this don't come along once in a lifetime. They're a hell of a lot rarer than that. Doctorates are common. Real discoveries—especially ones that shake paradigms—aren't."

"So are jobs and graduate fellowships," I returned. *"Cha-ching,* you know? Deadlines? Student loans?" *And promises.*

"Never mind that for a second," said Dr. Scheuer. "Just answer my question. This is what you want, isn't it? This is what you're really after."

"Of course it is," I said. "But—"

"And what would you do if you could do anything? If money and deadlines weren't a problem? Where would your next step take you?"

I pursed my lips as I thought. "I'd go to Germany, I think. Berlin. I need to see if I can backtrack and find more sources in the libraries there, older ones."

"That's what you think you should be doing, isn't it?"

It wasn't really a question; we both knew the answer. I had to swallow before I spoke. I felt the beginning of a tear pressuring the back of my eye. "Yes."

"Then do it. The deadline I can take care of. *Poof!* Consider it done. It may be a bit of a cliché, but it's no less true for that—when something's important, you make the time. The money's a little harder, but don't worry. I can talk to the grant people for you. We'll work something out. Somehow. We always do. Just . . . have a little faith, okay? There's always a way, my young friend. Always. And Jessie, this isn't a dilemma; this is your work, your real life's work. Now go on and do it, girl."

"I don't know if I can. Not alone. Not without David."

"You can, Jessie. You're alive, as much as that can hurt at times. Remember that. If you want to do something for David, do this. Do it for the both of you. Just like you promised."

"Dr. Scheuer, I don't know what to say."

"Try 'thank you,' Dear."

"Thank you! Oh, God, yes. Thank you!" My voice broke. I guess the emotional weight that had just been lifted was the same pressure that held the dam behind my eyes in place, because I had to wipe away an escaping tear. I knew it was going to be the first of many, but at least the others could wait until I hung up the bloody phone.

"You're very welcome. Now you go track down Sam's ghost. I'll make some calls."

"Thank you," I said again.

"And Jessie? Happy Christmas!"

By European standards, Paris and Berlin are a world apart. By American standards, they're right next-door. That's the difference between Americans and Europeans, I'd learned. Americans think a hundred years is a long time; Europeans think a hundred miles is a long way. I'd learned that the first time I took a road trip in England with David. Anyway, I'd have made it in no time if I could have hired a car, but, despite Dr. Scheuer's assurances, I didn't think my graduate student's budget could handle the strain, and I wasn't about to call Daddy for a loan. All the same, I did pretty well with those excellent European trains.

I had to hide a snicker when the German customs official on the train reached out his hand to me and requested, with polite efficiency: "Your papers, please." My dad, a fan of old war movies, would have loved that. David would have loved it, too. I imagined their smiles as I handed over my ticket and passport, and sudden nostalgia fell on me like a wave of sadness, as intense as it was unexpected. It's hard to be away from home at Christmas.

I found a seat and slumped down in it, hugging my arms close around my chest. All around me, families speaking French and German were traveling together for the holidays. For some reason I can't begin to explain, their merry laughter made me feel even more isolated. Thoughts of the Christmas Eve dinner I'd be missing troubled me. I could almost taste turkey roasted with white wine and butter and fresh sage and basil; my mouth watered for mashed potatoes and pepper gravy. I fancied I could smell the cinnamon-laced scent of pumpkin pie baking in the oven. I could almost hear Mom scolding or ordering about anyone hapless enough to come within earshot of her kitchen. When I closed my eyes, I saw my brother's kids opening presents by the tree while Daddy chased them around with a camcorder. He still used a camcorder, always, even though he had an iPhone.

I wondered if they'd set my place at the table even though I wouldn't be there. I wondered if they'd go to Midnight Mass without me—I was usually the one who dragged everyone along. I so love carols sung by the light of a thousand candles. . . .

A vintage recording of some old crooner singing *I'll be Home for Christmas* in English played on the train's loudspeakers, and I found myself humming along as the train rumbled through the cold German night.

I'll be home for Christmas, you can plan on me,
Please have snow, and mistletoe, and presents by the tree. . .

I tried not to think of home. I tried not to think of David. I ordered a coffee and tried to concentrate on cultural anthropology and paradigm-challenging ghost story motifs instead. It didn't work. I couldn't get that stupid carol out of my head. I was too lonely to sleep.

I thought of home. I thought of David. Mostly, I thought of David.

I reached into my bag and pulled my iPad out of my backpack, tapped the Photos icon, and swiped through images of holidays past—Christmas dinners, tree trimming, my cousins and me emptying stockings by the fireplace. The last pictures were of David and me. I paused at one favorite picture, a dual selfie we took in an airport. We were holding the First Married Christmas ornament.

Before I could stop myself, my hand reached down and touched David's face, a gentle motion, a sort of almost caress. The glass screen was hard and cold, not like David at all. I remembered.

I was pacing in David's smallish, upscale, semi-private office at the firm. I remembered it like it was yesterday, the window overlooking central London, his too-tidy desk, chairs for visitors, a glass wall and with an open door facing an open floor. Our suitcases were stacked near the door, along with a trunk holding the small mountain of gift bags. I was wearing my engagement ring, and every time I looked at it, I smiled. Even though David wasn't there. Even though he should have been. An hour ago.

I tried my best not to look at my watch again, but I did anyway. Maybe thirty seconds later, I looked again. We were seriously late.

An administrative assistant sat at her desk near the open glass door. I looked at her. "Anything?" It wasn't the first time I'd asked. It wasn't the tenth.

"Not yet," the woman said. "I'll let you know."

"Can you call him?

Somehow, she managed yet another of her perfectly professional smiles. "I'm afraid not. He's with the senior partners."

I bit my lower lip. "It's just . . . we're going to miss our flight. I mean, uh, holiday traffic and all. . . ."

"I'm sorry." She shrugged and spoke more gently. "The senior partners, you know."

At that very moment, at the end of the open floor, the light above an elevator chimed. The door opened. David came out like a bullet from a gun and sprinted toward me. "I'm sorry! I'm sorry!"

I scrambled for the bags. David helped. He nearly tripped over the trunk with the gift bags. It was chaos. I tried to glare at him, but I think I was too happy to manage it. "We were supposed to leave an hour ago!"

"I'm sorry," David said. "The senior partners, you know."

"I told her," the administrative assistant said to David. "I told you," she said to me.

"We're not going to make it!" I said.

David stopped and put his hands on my shoulders. "Jess, listen to me. We're going to make it."

"There's not another flight!"

"Jessie. We're going to make it. I promise." He smiled. "It'll be our Christmas miracle."

This time, I managed a perfectly good glare. "There's no such thing."

David stepped back, genuinely stunned. "Of course there is."

I didn't answer. I had luggage to wrestle with.

"Jessie," said David, "You love Christmas more than anyone."

"I love going home for Christmas. Which it's starting to look like I'm not gonna get to do."

"I'll get you home."

"Just get the cab, okay? Don't get a Lyft. A real London black cab will be faster. They never get lost."

"I mean, all those movies . . . one a night. Sometimes two."

I sighed. "I love Christmas. I love Christmas movies. Despite everything, including your wretched dancing, I still love you. But there's no such thing as miracles."

"My dancing is getting much better, thank you."

"Better," I acknowledged. "Which I guess is close to a miracle. But like I said, there's no such thing as miracles."

David started gathering the packages, including mine. "Isn't that rather the whole point of the thing?"

I grabbed the last of the bags, found the handle on my suitcase, and started moving. "C'mon!"

"Wait. Look, you almost forgot one. David held up the last bag, a gift bag, the one I'd nearly missed. It was the one with the First Married Christmas ornament. He pulled it out and showed it to me. Despite myself, I smiled.

Somehow, we got to Gatwick and made it through international security. We had to race to the gate. We didn't even stop for the bathroom. The flight was already boarding when we got to the gate.

"We made it!" David grinned. "Told you."

"You're lucky," I said, waggling a finger.

David kissed my cheek. We started toward the kiosk to show our boarding passes. "That I am," he agreed.

Just before I handed over my boarding pass, I noticed something. My heart stopped. "David! The ornament! I don't have it!"

He frowned. "You had it. I saw it."

"I don't have it now!"

"I'll get you another. We have a year, don't we?"

I was starting to cry. "I don't want another one. I want that one! I want the one you gave me on the day we . . . we. . . ." I couldn't finish. Dammit. I'm such an ugly crier.

David set his bags down and held me. I sobbed.

An announcement came over the PA system. "This is the final boarding call for Delta Flight 1625 to Atlanta."

"Jessie," David said, "we have to go. . . ."

And just at that moment, a young man jogged up to us. I looked up. He was holding the ornament bag. "Excuse me," he said. "I think this is yours? I think you left it at security."

I opened the bag and there it was, the First Married Christmas ornament. I laughed through my tears.

"See?" David said. "A Christmas miracle."

I wiped my nose and my tears on my sleeve. Christ but I was an ugly crier. "You're lucky."

"You're my miracle, Jessie."

I held him tight, and then I let him go so we could rush to the gate. "No I'm not."

"You're my Christmas miracle," said David. We handed over our boarding passes.

"There's no such thing."

Before we started down the jetway, David stopped me. "Here, Christmas selfie."

We huddled close, holding the ornament and its bag. David snapped the photo with his phone.

The picture I was looking at in the album was that same selfie we'd taken at the gate, David and me both grinning like a pair of idiots. I reached down and touched David's cold face on the screen one more time. There were more pictures, but I didn't have the heart to scroll through any more of them. Instead, I turned the tablet off and stared out the window at the darkness with sad eyes. My hand made a print on the fogged glass.

Before I realized what I was doing, I sang the last line of the carol softly to myself, along with the recording, my voice almost a whisper.

Christmas Eve will find me where the love light gleams,
I'll be home for Christmas, if only in my dreams.

My German was even worse than my French, but I made do.

I visited two university libraries and a public one. Thanks to librarians who spoke enough English to make up for my poor German, I found the references I needed. I had to call on a dictionary a time or two, and Google translate more than that, but I was able to read them on my own, even if it took longer by far than it should have. Once I got started, the language came back to me. Sort of.

I spent two days reading German urban legends and ghost stories. I found a total of four references that undeniably matched the elements in the Sam's ghost story motif—the correlations were too significant to ignore. The earliest dated from right after the Second World War.

The details were virtually identical in each report: a British Navy sailor appears on Christmas Eve, desperate to reach England. The time of day varied, but it was never earlier than around two p.m., and he always pulled his disappearing act at midnight. He was always desperate to get to London for Christmas. Often the driver had been to a funeral or something of the sort. The American wife's name, given in two of the four reports, was Emily. Allowing for minor spelling errors, the sailor's name was always Sam Prescott.

I found other references that seemed to fit (a few of them even mentioned Emily by name), but those didn't give the hitchhiking sailor's name. Others seemed to be "folk process" variants diluted as they were passed along from a friend of a friend to co-worker to third cousin twice removed. I recorded the references on post-its for future research, but I discarded them for now. For the moment, I would only concentrate on the reports where every detail matched.

Every detail, that is, save one: the location. I could almost trace the journey Sam's story took across Europe. I obviously couldn't find a reference for every year, but I found enough to establish a pattern. The earliest report was in Germany near the sea, a veritable dead-end. Unlike in France, I found no leads that might suggest a place to look elsewhere for earlier reports—although, if the facts checked out, I could contact researchers in neighboring countries and ask them to look for references later. The grad student and research librarian networks are amazing and quite astonishingly helpful. Meanwhile, the reports I found crossed Germany and

France in almost precise chronological order. Year after year, the story was repeated in a location closer and closer to England.

Like a lonely apparition hitchhiking toward London, toward home, getting a little closer each Christmas. . . .

I sighed and rubbed my temples.

This definitely didn't fit the urban legend model. The details, such as the sailor's name, should vary. The locations shouldn't make such a direct line from one point to another. They should spread out from the origin point, like ripples from the point where a stone is dropped in a pond. To search for an original source, a first author, one attempted to find the center of an ever-widening circle. One never simply followed a straight line. Not until now.

Most of the reports were sourced to a particular person who either claimed to have given Sam a ride, or to immediately know someone who had. Not a friend of a friend, a specific named person. That didn't fit the model, either. And for Heaven's sake, the reports shouldn't always happen on the same bloody day. Not even when the day was Christmas bloody Eve.

I chewed my lip and stared at my notes and my stack of photocopies for a good long while. Finally, I gathered my belongings and went back to my hotel room to order some supper and think.

I wished I could talk to David about the puzzle. He would have loved it. That made me want to cry all over again. Instead, I made myself focus.

Okay, the earliest reports dated back to the end of World War II. That meant that some of the sources might still be alive. If I could find them, they might be willing to be interviewed. After all, they obviously didn't mind talking. If they did, their tales wouldn't have made it to newspapers or books. If they talked to a friend or a tabloid reporter, maybe they'd talk to an academic. If I could get enough interviews, perhaps I could uncover the link.

Maybe I could learn where the story of Sam's ghost had originated, and why it spread in such an unusual, pattern-defying manner.

Even as I considered that possibility, another thought occurred to me. People would be hard to find. It might take weeks, or even months—*if* I got lucky. Even if good fortune was with me right away (a possibility; Europeans don't move around quite so much as we Americans), the holidays were less than a week away. They'd probably be too busy to talk to me, or too distracted to give me any useful information.

The trail in Germany seemed long cold, but in England it was still warm. Thanks to Jason, I knew that for a fact. Back there, I had more or less immediate access to two potentially original sources. I could start with the most recent and perhaps work up a hypothesis. Then, if all went well, I could backtrack through France and Germany and gather more information in the new year. All the way back to the first source, with any luck.

My next step was clear. I had to go back to London.

On the return train, I was too tired to read and too wired to sleep, which I must say is an absolutely wretched combination. The tinny speakers in the car again spewed canned holiday Muzak intermingled with a few sappy old standards, which had lulled most of the other passengers to sleep. I stared out at the darkness, seeing nothing, until a schmaltzy version of *Isn't It Romantic?* happened to play. It was one of the songs David and I used to play while we practiced our dancing. I wanted to smile and I wanted to cry, yes, and at the same time, because music makes you remember. I managed to do both.

Dance classes, it turned out, had one thing in common with regular old university classes: if you wanted to do well, there was a lot of homework. The was one major difference, however. It was a lot more pleasant than the reading I should have been doing, or the papers I should have been writing.

David held my left hand in his; his right was somewhere between my waist and the small of my back. He was singing along with the old standard we were streaming. He had a surprisingly nice voice. How could I be marrying this guy, when I didn't even know he could sing? The thought left me almost as soon as I'd thought it. *So there's more to discover—that's a good thing*, I decided. *May there always be new things to discover. . . .*

David sang as we danced. *"Isn't it romantic, music in the night—"*

"Ow!" I interjected. He'd stomped on my foot again.

"Isn't it ironic," David sang on, changing the lyrics. *"Her foot is in the wrong place—Ow!"* He stopped when I punched him in the shoulder.

"My foot was precisely where it belonged," I pointed out. "At the end of my leg. Which, I might add, was also in the right place. I'm supposed to step forward; you're supposed to go back. On the down beat."

"Right. Yes. Sorry, Jess."

"You are getting better, though."

"I am, aren't I?" He pulled me close. We were still dancing, slow and close. It wasn't the lesson we'd learned in class, it was more of a swaying hug, but I liked it all the same. David smelled like sandalwood, wine, and his own natural, salty musk. I drank in his scent and smiled as I rested my head against his chest.

"You are. In another couple of years, you'll be a regular Fred Astaire."

"You'll be my Ginger?"

"Backwards and in heels," I promised him. "Always."

"Do you even own heels, then?"

"Do you want to keep dancing or what?"

"I do," said David.

"Good," I said. "Because God knows you need the practice. Unless you want me limping to our honeymoon suite."

"I'll carry you. Besides, we have plenty of time. It only takes, what? Ten-thousand hours to master something? We have forever."

"Mmmm. I like that. But we only have three months till the wedding."

"Ah, right. Well, I'd best hurry, then. And I suppose we'd best keep practicing, wouldn't you say?" He stopped and pushed me gently away. "But let's wait till the next song, why don't we?"

I rolled my eyes. David had a quirk. Well, he had many, but I'm thinking of one specific one. No matter how much we practiced, be it in class or at home, David would never dance all the way through a whole song. He'd always stop before the last verse.

"Again?"

"Again," he confirmed.

"Just a little more? I like this song. Even when you mess up the lyrics."

"Especially when I mess up the lyrics."

"I admit nothing."

I reached out my arms for him, but he stepped back. "No, no, no. You know the rule. If we dance through the whole song, it counts as a dance. And we've agreed, haven't we? We'll have our first dance on our wedding night."

"You're silly." I reached out and hugged him close, careful not to move so it wouldn't count as a dance. I felt positively Baptist.

"That's why you love me," said David. "Because I'm silly."

"I had been wondering. And I guess it's good we saved *something* for the wedding night."

The next song started, and we danced again. David didn't step on my feet even once. Not that night, anyway.

The funny thing is, when our wedding night finally came, we never even had that first dance. We didn't dance at all, in fact. There was a bit of an accident, you see.

We married in the gardens behind David's parents' cottage close to Oxford, as lovely and charming a story-book place as you can imagine. The house was of stacked stone and white plaster, and every window sported boxes heavy with flowers. The gardens were green and ripe with luscious color. Truly, it saved us a fortune in decorating, just the thing for our budgets. Oh, Daddy would have thrown us a huge wedding back home in Alabama, but that would have taken so much longer to plan, and there was the issue of coordinating the travel with demands of my classes and David's new job. Why, the wedding itself would have eaten up most of our available time; our Honeymoon would have been a long weekend at best, which is just not the best way to see the Greek Islands for the first time. Or to start a marriage. Of course, the real truth is that a wedding in Oxford could be arranged so much more quickly, and David and I wanted to be married as soon as possible. When one finds the one they want to live happily ever after with, well, they want to start going about it as quickly as possible, don't they? Besides, we were going to spend Christmases with my family, most of them, anyway, and I'd likely get Thanksgivings as well, since that's not really a thing in England, so it seemed only fair.

I made sure David didn't see my gown until the actual moment. It worked—he actually gasped when I appeared. A string quartet played softly as I walked down a path strewn with bright flower petals. David stood with Jason and his father, and one of my little cousins who served as ring bearer. I'd wanted them to go casual, but David had insisted on tuxedos. I'll admit he made the right call. His sandy-brown hair was trimmed and slicked back. He looked magnificent. The priest was an old friend of David's family. He smiled fondly as we gathered for the sacred moment, and I could just tell his warmth was genuine. We wrote our own vows, and we made ourselves cry as we read them. Somehow, we got through them.

It took far, far longer to take all the pictures than I would have thought possible. By the time we finally got inside, most of the food was gone. I'd known Mom and Daddy would come, of course, and we'd invited the others just to be polite. They came, all of them. Every aunt and uncle, every single cousin. Well, most of them. More old friends than I could count. Even my third-grade teacher. They all came all the way to England, all of them, to see me marry David. With all sincerity, I think we must have temporarily reduced the population of the state of Alabama by at least half. There were so very many people to catch up with, so many necks to hug! Then there was a cake to cut, and toasts, and champagne to drink.

Somewhere along the way, David and Jason took some of my male cousins outside to show them some of the finer points of rugby and soccer; the only foot-involved sport any of my Alabama kin knew was good old 'mericun football. It did not go well. Twenty minutes or so later, David came back inside, limping, his arms draped around Jason and my cousin Jack's necks. He'd turned his ankle but good. His mother and I took him to his old room to ice his foot and wrap it in an Ace bandage. We even managed to do it without laughing. Well, not too much, anyway. David's father wanted to give him one of his canes, but David insisted it wasn't quite that bad.

And we had to rush to Heathrow to catch our flight.

Our driver had just turned on to the A40 when David sat up abruptly. His happy smile turned into a gasp and his eyes popped open like a pair of window shades. "Jessie! Our dance!"

I lifted my head off my new husband's shoulder and smiled. "I'm not sure you were quite up to that, my love."

"But . . . blimey!" Yes, my fellow Americans, he actually said blimey. "We missed it, didn't we?"

"We missed our first dance. And because of soccer."

"Football."

"Yes, that's precisely the issue."

He smiled and then he sang, *"Isn't it ironic?"*

"And after all those lessons and all my bruised feet."

"I believe I am paid back."

I nodded. "Karma is satisfied."

"We can have our first dance in Greece," David suggested. "It'll be a honeymoon dance."

"On that foot? Ha. Not likely."

"Blimey and blimey all over again. What about all those hikes we'd planned?"

I smiled my best bad girl smile and looked up at him through my lashes. "We'll think of something to pass the time."

"Perhaps we can have a first hop."

"I've already had a few of those," I reminded him. "Remember all the bruised feet?"

"No, wait! I have a better idea. We'll do it at Christmas, when we go to Alabama." He tried to do a southern accent when he said Alabama. He failed miserably. My English accent is *much* better, even if he'd never admit it. "We'll have a traditional Christmas hoedown."

"I'm telling you. That's still not a thing."

"What about a Christmas hootenanny?"

"Is that different?" I asked him.

"How on earth should I know?"

"I'm pretty sure that's not a thing either."

"Not even in Alabama?"

"Not anywhere. Especially not in Alabama."

"Well, we'll just have to start our very own tradition, won't we?" David declared. "The very first Alabama Christmas Hoedown."

"Not hootenanny?"

"We'll have both. Both at once! Yes! The first ever and first annual Alabama Christmas Hoedown and Hootenanny. And I'm sure your whole family will come. Even the many cousins."

"That's probably true," I admitted.

David nodded. "And we'll have our first dance there, won't we?" He sang, more or less to the tune of *Isn't it Romantic* again.

"Isn't it ironic,
dancing at a Christmas hoedown in the night—"

"I don't think they play the kind of music we've been practicing to at hoedowns. Or hootenannies either, for that matter. Christmas or otherwise."

"How do you know?"

"I'm pretty sure."

"I thought you said it wasn't thing. Christmas hoe-downs *or* hootenannies."

"They're not. I'm pretty sure."

"Well then. If they're not a thing, why, we can make them whatever we want, can't we? We're inventing the things, after all. We're the very founders of the glorious new holiday tradition. If we can work in some disco as well, so much the better."

I threw my head back and laughed. "I can't argue with that."

"Then it's settled. We'll have our first dance in Alabama, when we go home for Christmas."

"We will," I agreed.

We didn't.

6

The Reluctant Witness

elaxing at my own breakfast table in my own kitchen in my own tiny, familiar, dumpy flat, I made myself a pot of coffee and drank it out of my own favorite mug. Then I rang Jason to get Colm's phone number. Jason proved only too happy to oblige me. I didn't even detect a hint of smugness. After that, things didn't go so well.

"Hi," I began when Colm answered. I tapped my well-chewed pencil on my notepad as I spoke. "This is Jessie Malone, Jason Cook's friend. Uh, I don't know if you remember meeting me at the pub?"

"Of course I do, Jessie girl! How are you, then?"

We exchanged seasonal pleasantries before I got down to business. "Listen, Colm," I transitioned, "I hate to bother you on a Sunday, or at all, really, but do you think I might be able to ask you a favor?"

"Why, of course, Jessie. What can I do for you?"

"I don't know if Jason told you, but I'm working on my Ph.D. in Cultural Anthropology. My dissertation is on urban legends. . . ."

"Ah, Jason told me all about it, didn't he?" said Colm. "That's why we thought you'd be interested in Mickey's tale about Sam's ghost."

I shifted the phone in my grip and took a deep breath. "Yeah. Uh, Jason was right." How I hated those words! Suppressing a smile, I continued. "Anyway. I'd like to follow up on the story of Sam's ghost. I think it might be important. You see, it doesn't fit the model of how these things usually work—"

"Of course not, Jessie," Colm interrupted me. "It's true, not a story!"

I gave up holding back the smile and let it blossom. "Well, do you think I might talk to Mickey? Interview him? About Sam."

"Ah," said Colm. "I see. No. No, I'm afraid that won't be possible."

That thought had never occurred to me. I'd been sure that I'd be able to talk to at least one original source. I swallowed, but my voice abandoned me. A simple "Oh" was all I managed.

"Poor missy," Colm said with an almost comically exaggerated sigh. "I'm glad you're at least trying to hide the disappointment in your voice. I'm not sure I could handle it if you turned it on me full force!"

"I'm sorry. I didn't mean . . . I just—"

"It's all right then, sure," said Colm. "I should have told you before. Mickey, he doesn't exactly like to talk about what happened to him that Christmas Eve, does he? And can you blame him? He thinks people will try to lock him right up in Bedlam, sure."

"He told you," I pointed out.

"He told his Mum," Colm reminded me.

"Oh," I said again. We were both silent for an uncomfortable moment. Breathing sounds awfully loud over the phone when no one's speaking.

"Look," Colm said at last. "I'll talk to him, yes? I can't promise anything, no, but maybe if I ask him just right, and tell him a little about you. About how you promised not to laugh, or to take him to some university laboratory so that you can snigger behind mirrored glass while he answers a great lot of embarrassing questions about his dreams, his mum, and his sex life. Er, you *do* promise that, yes?"

"Of course!"

"I'll talk to him, then. I'll see him over Christmas, won't I? I'll ply him with some mulled wine, sure. Maybe I can change his mind. But no promises, now, Missy. You can understand why he'd be a mite sensitive now, can't you, Jessie?"

"I can. Thanks, Colm. Thanks anyway."

"But Jessie, be ready for disappointment. Mickey's not going to be happy when he hears I've been telling his tale. Even though it's a grand one. I doubt he'll want to talk to you."

I hung up the phone and stared at the wall. I'd failed.

I guess the rational part of my brain knew even then that I had other avenues to explore, but right then I just plain wanted to sulk, so I indulged the mood and let disproportionate disappointment fall on me like a rainstorm. I huddled down on my couch, the one where I used to sit with David, and let the misery take me. I sat with my knees under my chin and my arms wrapped around my legs. I was cold but I didn't do anything about that, either. Grief was my blanket. I couldn't even cry. Dr. Scheuer was going to be so disappointed. David would be so disappointed. I'd failed him, too.

David.

I hadn't meant to, not when I needed to be working, but I'd left the door wide open, and memory marched right in, bringing sorrow with it.

I'd been sitting on that same couch, in almost the same exact position. Our Christmas tree stood in the corner. We'd almost finished decorating it. Almost. It made the tiny space even tinier, but somehow, we made it homey and charming all the same.

David was rushing about, packing his suitcase and trying to remember what he'd forgotten. It was his wedding ring, as it turned out, and of course he wound up leaving without it. I was sipping a cup of coffee. I'd made it too strong and left it on the burner too long; it was bitter. I drank it anyway. I thought about adding milk. I didn't.

"I wish you didn't have to go. Not at Christmas."

David sighed without looking at me. "Tell the senior partners, why don't you?"

"I just will! Here, give me your phone—"

David stopped and turned to me. "Whoa! Slow down. I'd like to keep my job, thank you very much indeed. And perhaps get that bloody promotion finally. . . ."

I closed my eyes and looked down. I took a deep breath and let it out before I spoke. "David, please, the weather. . . ."

David kissed me on the forehead. I always loved when he did that.

"Jessie. Listen to me. It's just a quick meeting. Right? I'll be back. Before Christmas."

"We barely even had a honeymoon."

David smiled. "That's all we've ever had. I'll be home, and in plenty of time to make our flight. Okay? We'll have our first ever and first annual Alabama Christmas Hoedown and Hootenanny. We'll have our first dance, Jessie. All the way to the end."

"You better." It was one of my better pouts, if I do say so, but he'd turned away.

"C'mon. Help me hang the last ornament?"

I looked up. David was holding the First Married Christmas ornament he'd given me. The one I'd almost lost at airport security the year before. The one I treasured even more than my rings, the more usual symbols of our love and promises. He was still smiling, and his eyes were wide and bright.

I shook my head. I didn't get up.

"Jessie, c'mon, eh? It's finally time to hang it, isn't it?"

I shook my head again. "No."

David looked back at me, surprised, his eyebrows raised.

"No," I said again. "We'll hang it when you get back."

"Jess—"

"No. It's not our first married Christmas. Not yet. Not till you come home."

David set the ornament down, carefully, among the greenery that we'd arranged to decorate the fireplace mantel. He smiled. "I'll come home, Jessie, and in plenty of time to get you home, okay? For Christmas. I promise."

He didn't, of course.

He kissed me again, on the lips and then the forehead, just the way I liked. It was the last time he kissed me like that, as it turned out. It was the last time he kissed me at all.

I waited. I was pacing, waiting for him to call and tell me he was on his way. I paced for a long time. More than once, I stopped to touch the First Married Christmas ornament in its place on the mantle, waiting, wishing I was touching David's face instead.

I paced some more. I waited. It was a long time before the phone rang at last. I raced to answer it. "David?"

"Jess, I'm at the Glasgow airport, but it's no good. The snow up here's too bad. All the flights are canceled."

"I knew it. Oh, David!"

"Jessie, no, it's okay. I've hired a car. I'll make it."

"From Scotland? David!"

He laughed. "Hey, Jess, the whole bloody island's not much bigger than Alabama, right? I'll be there in a jiff."

His laughter didn't convince me. "David, the weather!"

"Jessie, I'll be home. For Christmas. We'll hang the ornament. We'll make our flight. We'll have our first dance."

"All the way to the end?"

"All the way to the end. I love you."

"Be careful. I love you, too."

I'm glad that's the last thing we said to each other. That's something, anyway. I wish I'd tried harder to stop him. I wish I'd convinced him to spend the night. I wish I'd been braver, that I'd been strong enough to find the words. I didn't, though. I wanted him home too badly. I

wanted us to hang the First Married Christmas ornament together. I'd saved a bough specially for it. At least
we said I love you.

I waited through the day and long into the night.
I tried to sleep a little, but that was no good. I tried to
work, but that was no good, either. Mostly, I paced. I
stopped to touch the First Married Christmas ornament
so many times I had to wipe it clean of my fingerprints.

I was back on that damn couch, wrapped in a blanket,
when the call came at last. I ran to it, even though . . . even
though a part of me already knew. "David?"

It wasn't, of course.

There had been an accident. Given the icy roads, it
had taken a long time for the ambulance to reach him.
David was dead before they could get him to a hospital.
I don't even remember the words. I was numb. My world
had ended, utterly and forever, and I couldn't even cry.

I don't remember much about the days that followed. Somehow, arrangements were made, people
notified. I barely even remember the funeral. It was a
graveyard service, very simple. David would have wanted
that. The priest who'd officiated at our wedding, the old
friend of his family's, spoke words under gloomy skies.
I watched with dead eyes through a black veil. I can't
recall a single thing he said. I'm told that David's sister
sang his favorite hymn. I hadn't even known he'd had a
favorite hymn.

A few more days passed. I was back in our flat. All the guests had been shooed away, and all the casserole dishes were empty. I hadn't even known they knew about casseroles here in England. Or maybe that was something my relatives from the States had provided. They'd all come, of course. I don't even know.

I was tidying, because I had to do something, and God knows the sleep and work things still weren't happening. I found the First Married Christmas ornament, still in its place on the mantel. The greenery surrounding it was already turning brown. I lifted it carefully by its hook. I wiped away another fingerprint. I turned. The bough I'd saved was still bare, empty and waiting. I looked at it.

I couldn't hang it. I couldn't make myself do it. Not alone, not without David.

And that's when the tears came at last, a storm of sorrow that brought rage with it, thunder with the rain. I took the ornament and ran to a window on the far side of the tiny room. I flung it open and screamed with raw fury. With something between a scream and a grunt, I threw the ornament, as hard as I could, with all the might I could muster. It didn't even make it across the alley. It didn't even shatter in a satisfying way. It hit the side of a metal rubbish bin and cracked with a delicate tink.

And then it was gone, that first symbol of our love and promises, of our hopes for the future, that last piece of David that I'd had left to hold on to. Just like that, it was gone. Gone forever.

Our First Married Christmas ornament was broken and lost.

I slid down to the floor, sobbing and screaming until my throat was raw.

I spent the rest of the day moping around the flat. I couldn't believe it. All this work, only to hit an apparent dead end where I'd thought to find a sure thing. I didn't get dressed. I pulled a reference book off the shelf, but I never opened it. I sat in my robe in front of the TV, but I didn't even bother to turn it on. I didn't accomplish a darn thing, unless you consider drinking three glasses of wine constructive. I didn't even think. I wrapped depression around me like a blanket and sat there, quiet and alone. I'd thought I'd faced the grief, I'd thought I was healing. But I hadn't, and I wasn't, not really.

Why didn't you come back to me, David? Why didn't you come home?

We'd never hung our ornament. We'd never danced our first dance. Now we never would. Never wait for the right moment. Those never come.

I'd never been able to let go. I'd never been able to say goodbye. David haunted me.

I was still there on my threadbare little sofa, trying to decide where numb sadness is in the stages of grief, when the phone rang. I didn't answer it, but the caller hung up when the machine clicked on. Seconds later, the phone started ringing again. I still couldn't muster the energy to answer. Again the machine started its recorded greeting; again the caller hung up. And called back. I sighed. Realizing that whoever it was wasn't going to give up and leave me alone, I finally surrendered. If it turned out to be a telemarketer, heads would roll.

"Hello?"

"Hey, baby girl."

"Hi, Daddy." I should have guessed. I should have let it ring; I wasn't in the mood. But no, that wouldn't have worked. He'd have kept on calling until, sooner or later, he wore me down.

"Did I call at a better time? The time zones, I mean. I kept getting your machine."

"Sorry, Daddy, I was in the tub," I lied.

"Ah. Should have known. Big plans tonight?"

"Just work, Daddy."

"I see. Relaxing, then? Herbal soap and bubbles? Wine and candles?"

That's not a bad idea. "Just like Mom likes," I hedged.

"Well, I got the time right, didn't I? Better this time?"

"Much, thanks."

"You don't sound good."

"I'm just a little tired, Daddy, that's all. Really. I've just got so much to do—"

"Stress isn't healthy," he said. "Especially at the holidays. Sounds like you need a break, baby girl."

I sighed. *Here it comes.*

"Why don't you come home, Jessie? For Christmas. Everyone wants to see you. It's just not Christmas if the whole family isn't there, baby."

I heard the pain in his voice, and it broke my heart. Daddy was happiest when we were all together; he always had been. The great sadness of his life was working so hard to build a structure, a home and a stable family, that was meant to fall apart after twenty years or so. Kids are meant to grow up and move away, in our culture at least, so they can face their own heartbreak in time, but Daddy longed for the comfort of permanence.

I used to long for that, too. But that was . . . that was before. Before David. A part of me wanted to be home, ached for it, really, but I just wasn't ready. Not yet. Maybe I never would be. Maybe I was like Sam. Doomed to wander but never to arrive.

"Daddy, we talked about this. I *can't.*"

"You're sure? Honey, when something's important, you make time." I'd been hearing that a lot lately. "What's more important than being with the people who love you at Christmas?"

"My work? My Ph.D.? All that education you've been paying for? Not losing my grant and fellowship?" I counted each item off on my fingers as I made the list. *And the fact that I promised David. . . .*

And because we never hung our First Married Christmas Ornament, and because I just can't stand to look at a tree without it, and because we never had our dance. . . .

It hurts too much, too damn much. That's why I never come home, Daddy. You see that, don't you?

"I know all that, Jessie girl. I do. I just wish you'd think about it, okay? So does Mom. We all do."

"I have, Daddy, believe me. You know I want to, right? You know how much I miss you. I miss you all so much! But Christmas, Daddy, in the end it's just another day. There'll be others. Lots of them. This is my once-in-a-lifetime chance. I have to finish, Daddy. I have to."

I promised David, Daddy. I promised him. And I'm hurting. I'm hurting too, too, too damn much.

"I know you do, Honey. I know. And we're proud of you. I know you can do whatever you set your mind to, and I know you make good decisions. But we'll miss you, and we'll be thinking about you."

"Thank you, Daddy," I said, meaning more than the words were meant to contain.

"Good luck. Love you, baby."

"I love you, too, Daddy."

Well, I thought as I hung up the phone. *That didn't go as badly as I expected.*

The sadness and the ache of loneliness fell on me again, but so did an unexpected wave of fierce determination. Daddy had faith in me. That faith was stronger than his need to have his family together. David had believed in me, too. Thinking of that, I reached for the phone again. I'd hit a roadblock, but I certainly hadn't come to the end of the journey. Not by a long shot. I mouthed a silent prayer that Jason wasn't already on a plane heading home to America for the holidays. When was he supposed to leave again?

Luck was with me. He answered on the third ring. "Hello?"

"Hey, Jason," I began. "It's me. Listen, do you happen to have that cabbie's number handy? The one who picked up Sam's ghost?"

7

The Chatty Cabbie

here is something amazing about real London Black Cab drivers. They know everything. I don't mean everything in some kind of hyperbolic or metaphorical sense. I mean seriously, *everything*. Well, about the layout of London, anyway.

London is one of the largest and oldest cities on the planet. Its twisting, mind-numbing labyrinth of streets and alleys date back to a time when city planners and civil engineers were men strong enough to knock down ancient trees with axes of stone or bronze. I've heard it said that there are more streets in London and its suburbs than there are names in the New York City phone book. I believe it. To become a licensed cabbie in London, one must know them all, every street and alley, as well as all the routes, places of interest, and street numbers. They call it the Knowledge. One literally has to study for years before attempting even the first of the Knowledge tests required to become a London cabbie.

When I first visited London on a school trip, I decided to put the famous Knowledge to the test. I asked for an obscure Indian restaurant in a far suburban area. The cabbie not only knew the place, he even knew the menu. As we drove, he told me what to order and what to avoid. I've never once heard tell of anyone stumping a London cabbie—some things, apparently, are too unbelievable even for urban legend.

I've been told that autopsies conducted on deceased cabbies had actually revealed physical changes in the brain. Apparently, the very act of learning the Knowledge formed new neural pathways. *Hmmm*. I wonder if that's true, or if it's just another urban myth. That just might be a subject to follow up on for study. Later. Yes, definitely later.

There are two kinds of cabbies in London. There are the quiet ones who ask your destination and take you there in silence with little fuss. Then there are the chatty ones, the ones who fill the ride with questions about you and your home, and who will both amaze and delight you with odd trivia and fascinating details about the city around you as you whiz through its bustling streets. Like I said, they know *everything*. A chatty cabbie is a treasure, one of the great joys of London. Jason's friend Trevor Longbottom was one such.

We met at a chippy between the Tottenham Court tube station and the bookshops along Charing Cross Road. If a chatty cabbie is one of London's treasures, real fish and chips are another. This place still served them properly, piping hot and wrapped in newspaper, gloriously greasy, and with plenty of good malt vinegar available on the side. I bought Mr. Longbottom his lunch and a pint to wash it down. That seemed to endear me to him.

Mr. Longbottom wore a crisply pressed white shirt with a burgundy necktie under a blue blazer with polished brass buttons. He'd parted his thinning hair on the side; not to hide his bald spot but simply to make the best use of what he had. He had a real honest-to-God waxed handlebar moustache that curled at the ends. As we dined, I learned a little of his life story. A staunch royalist, he'd had the honor of serving Queen and country in Her Majesty's armed forces in India before retiring and studying to become a cabbie.

We'd just finished our lunch when I turned the subject to Sam's ghost. Unlike Colm's cousin Mickey, Mr. Longbottom was only too happy to tell me what had happened on Christmas Eve six years earlier. I went and bought us two more pints. When I returned with the full glasses, he leaned back in his chair and pressed his fingers together. Now came the fateful moment. Would his account match the others?

"So how much did young Master Cook already tell you, then?" He spoke with just a hint of Cockney in his voice, enough to make me guess that he'd been born within the so-called "square mile" of the original city of old London. I'd been in the city just long enough to start distinguishing between the various local urban accents.

"Not too much," I replied. "Just the basic outline, really. I'd love to hear it from you, though. In your own words."

"I don't blame you a bit," Mr. Longbottom said with an understanding nod. "I tell a much better story than our young Master Jason. Shall I give it to you now?"

"Would you mind if I record this?"

"Not in the least."

I tapped my phone's app to start the recording. "May I ask you a question first?"

"Certainly," he said.

"Do you happen to know a man named Mickey Smythe? Or Colm Jameson?"

Mr. Longbottom laughed. "Ah, didn't your mate Jason ask me that very same question? I'll have to give you the same answer I gave him. London's a big town, Missy. No matter what you Americans might think, we don't all know each other."

"Of course," I said, genuinely embarrassed. It didn't seem like a good idea to explain the real reason why I'd asked. "Sorry about that."

"Think nothing of it. Shall I begin?"

"Please do."

"Well then," he started, "it was typical Christmas weather here in London. That is to say, it was cold, misty, and raining."

"How exactly is that different from typical London weather during the rest of the year?" I asked with, I confess, a bit of a smirk.

"As to that," he said, giving me a mock glare and a wink, "a storyteller is much less likely to be interrupted on Christmas, ducks."

"Oh. Sorry," I said, hiding my smile behind my hand. "I'll listen quietly."

"See that you do," he said. He gave me a glare, but he softened it with another friendly wink. "Now then, as I was saying. It was a rainy night, cold and miserable, for all that it was Christmas Eve. I was driving that afternoon. Oh, I wanted to be back home, sure, of course I did, but people need to get places, even on the holiday, don't they? And someone has to get them there, don't they? And with the wife gone, well, it might as well be me, I expect. A little company is good at the holiday, even when it's the company of strangers."

I nodded. "I understand."

"Do you? Yes, I think you might."

"So what happened?"

"Well then," he continued, "it couldn't have been much past three in the afternoon, but it was already getting close on to dark, what with the weather and the shorter days and all. I was driving down along Bankside down by the old docks."

"Close to the river?"

His lip twitched, the beginning of a smile. "And where else would there be docks, then?"

I grinned. "Right. Sorry."

"Nothing of it," Mr. Longbottom said with a chuckle. "To continue, I was driving along, having just deposited a fare on her very doorstep, safe and as dry as can be expected given the rain, and I was making my way back towards the bridge to cross back over to this side of the river. Just then, all of a sudden like, I saw a man standing right in front of me, waving me down. Why, I had to slam me brakes to keep from runnin' right over the chap, didn't I?"

"Do you remember where you were? Sorry, I don't mean to interrupt—"

"That's all right, Missy," he said patiently. "And of course I do. Remember, I mean." He tapped the side of his forehead with his index finger and smiled. "It's the Knowledge, isn't it? I was right on Clink Street, sure. Just a block or so away from Winchester House. You know that old ruin?"

I nodded. "Down near the Globe Theatre, right?"

"Just so."

A thought occurred to me. "Tell me," I said. "Is there a pub close to there called The Admiral's Men?"

"Of course there is, ducks. It's just right down the hill, isn't it?"

So already Mr. Longbottom's account had a link in common with Colm's. He was right near the same place where Colm said Mickey had picked up Sam. Within a few city blocks at the very least. And on Christmas Eve, too. My heartbeat quickened a bit. This is it, I thought to myself. I'm actually talking to an original source, a real, actual original source, an author of an urban legend, or an episode variation, anyway.

Oh my God, this is it!

"So what happened?" I asked again.

"I slammed me brakes, just to keep from runnin' over the chap, didn't I? Couldn't have stopped more than a foot or two away from where he stood, right there in the middle of the road, waving his fool arms over his head like he was trying to flag down an airplane or a ship at sea.

"No sooner did I stop than he ran around and hopped right into the back seat behind me. 'Thank God!' says he. 'I was beginning t'think nobody was going to stop for me!'

"My cab felt dastardly cold all of a sudden and I shivered, although I suppose that was just the wind howling the chill in. Although I can't say it seemed all that much warmer even when he pulled the door closed. I shrugged back at him, saying, 'Well, it's Christmas, me lad, isn't it? I suppose people are just in a hurry to get themselves on home, and don't think no never mind about others, do they?'

"The boy just shook his head. 'You'd think that's the time when people would think the most about others, then, wouldn't you?'

"'I suppose so at that,' I agreed. 'Now then, let's see about getting you where you need to be, what? Where to?' The lad, he gives me an address way up in Hampstead."

"Do you remember the address?" I asked Mr. Longbottom.

"Of course I do, ducks," he said, smiling and tapping his forehead again. "Like I told you. It's the Knowledge, isn't it? The address he gave me was number 39 Marley Lane. You can take that to the bank. Now then, as I was saying. So I started off that way, but Hampstead was a pretty far piece to go, especially with the awful weather."

Hampstead. Another link with Mickey's account. There must be a connection between them. I made a note.

"Tell me," I said, "Do you remember what the man was wearing?"

"You bet I do. It was one of those baggy uniforms like they used to wear in the Royal Navy. Petty Officer, I think, though I won't swear to it. I'm not really too sharp with all that nautical stuff, you know. I did my time in Her Majesty's service, sure, but I did it safe on good old terra firma, didn't I?"

"Did you have a chance to talk to him at all?" I prompted.

"That I did. Hampstead's a bit of a drive, you know, even on Christmas Eve when the traffic's a mite lighter, so we had plenty of time to have ourselves a nice chat. He didn't tell me much about himself, though; mostly he wanted to talk about this pretty American girl he'd married. A girl called Emily. I remember it like it was yesterday. He spoke those words like he could taste 'em, like every syllable was the gentlest caress. Emily Prescott, née Wilson. That's a pretty name, isn't it?"

I nodded. "Did he tell you his own name?" I asked, and instantly regretted it. *Stop that,* I admonished myself. *You're influencing the tale. Just like with the uniform question.*

"He certainly did. It was Sam Prescott."

Sam! That was it, another telling detail, concrete and absolutely unambiguous, to link his account with the others. If my pulse had quickened before, now it roared, like a racecar screaming away from the starting line. I could practically smell the burning rubber, a scent we Alabama girls know well.

Mr. Longbottom must have noticed my reaction, because his eyes narrowed with concern. "Are you all right, Missy? You look like you've seen a ghost!" We both smiled at his little joke.

"Sorry," I said. I had to look away from his worried gaze. "I was just enjoying the story. Please continue?"

He nodded. "Of course. Well, we drove through that cold, wet mess, Sam alternately watching the city through the mist as we passed and telling me more about his American girl. They hadn't been married long before he'd had to ship out, you know, but he'd promised her he'd be home for Christmas."

The next key detail. And, oh my God! From an actual original source! Not a friend of a friend!

"Well, I told him not to worry a bit, because I'd have him home before he could whistle all the verses of *The Twelve Days of Christmas*. Now then, it wasn't too long before we made it up to Hampstead, and didn't I take him right straight to the address he'd given me? It was one of those new places they were throwing up there about thirty years back. Those plain, ugly brick places. Do you know the ones?"

I shook my head. "I've not been up there much," I confessed.

"Ah. Sure, I wouldn't bother. There're some pretty enough spots up there, a good pub or two, some galleries and arty stuff if that's your pleasure, and there's the museums and the bookshops, of course. There's some protected parkland, which is nice enough. And there's them as likes the Bohemian character up there, so each to his own, as it were. 'Course, it's not too far out if you take the tube, not that I'd recommend that as a cabbie, mind, and you can't really say you've had the complete London experience without it.

"But as I was saying. I pulled up right in front of the address our young Sam had given me, but he just stared, with a look of confusion and, I don't mind saying, something like absolute despair in his eyes. 'This can't be right!' says he.

"'Sure, this is the address you gave me,' says I. 'Are you certain this isn't the place? Didn't you say you'd only been here the once, and only for a wink or two before you shipped out?'

"'Wouldn't I know my own home, then?' says he.

And so it went. The story I'd heard so many times I could tell it by heart. They circled. They came back. They lathered, they rinsed, they repeated.

"We drove," Trevor told me, "and daylight turned to twilight, and twilight faded to darkness. I didn't mind too much, of course. The meter was running, wasn't it? Of course, I'd have given the boy a bit of a discount. What with it being Christmas and all, you know. That is, if I could ever get him out of my cab.

"Hampstead's a twisting little place, but it's just that. Little, I mean. Well, little enough that you can cover every foot and yard of every last street and alley of it in a fairly short period of time. We didn't find the place where that boy's Emily was waiting for him. Worse, it was getting late. Close to midnight it was. I didn't have a pretty wife waiting for me, not anymore, may God rest her dear soul, but me old Dad would be expecting me bright and early in the morning, along with me sisters. For Christmas Day, you understand."

"Of course," I said with a nod. I finished the last of my ale and set the empty pint glass down on the table. "So what did you do?"

"That boy Sam, he was getting pretty close to frantic by then, let me tell you, ducks. He just kept saying, 'I promised her! I promised her I'd be home for Christmas! I promised her!' We were just pulling back around to the address he'd given me to start with, so I pulled over. Maybe somebody would know this Emily, or something useful, anyway. The lights were still on.

"It was raining harder then, so I huddled over and pulled my coat over my head as I ran to the door. I rapped the brass knocker three times. Right away, I heard the sounds of someone stirring 'round. The door opened. A chap stood there, still dressed even given the late hour.

"'Hello there,' says he. 'You brought Sam, did you? I've been waiting up.'

"'So I do have the right address,' says I.

"The man laughed like I'd just told the best joke in the whole world. 'Someone tries to bring a sailor called Sam here to his wife every year on Christmas Eve,' says he. 'I've learned to wait up; it's kind of a holiday tradition for the missus and me. Been happening for years now.'

When he spoke those words, sure, my jaw nearly dropped down to the cold concrete floor of his porch. 'But that can't be!' says I.

"The man gave me a smile and a shrug, he did. 'You can go on home now, sir. I think you'll find when you get back to your cab that your young Sam has disappeared.'

"The man was right. When I got back to my cab, Sam was gone. How he managed to slip away without one of us seeing him, well, that I can't say, any more than I can say how he managed to open and close the cab door without me hearing it. Believe me, I looked good and well, seein' as to how the bilker had stiffed me for the fare! And I never saw hide nor hair of him again.

"And that, Miss Jessie Malone, is a true story. It actually happened just like I told you, and that's a fact I'll swear before God and all the saints and angels. Now then. What do you make of it?"

"It's . . . it's incredible, Mr. Longbottom."

"Call me Trevor, ducks. Please."

"Trevor. There's something else I have to ask. This is a little awkward."

Trevor lifted his eyebrows. "Then to save you asking, there's no history of mental illness, either. Not in me nor me family. Nor anything of the sort. And I never, ever take even a sip of a drink when I'm to be driving." Trevor winked. I shifted in my seat, embarrassed. "Your mate Jason already asked, he did. He knew you'd want to know."

"Of course. Sorry about that. I'm just being thorough."

Trevor leaned back and smiled knowingly. "Of course you are. Now. Why is that?"

"Because your account isn't the first I've heard."

"I didn't think so," said Trevor. "And all the details match, don't they? Or close enough. Our Jason said you'd want to know that, too. The science, after all. Now then. Tell me what's troubling you."

"Well . . . urban legends aren't supposed to work like this!" I sighed. I shouldn't have said that. No self-respecting cultural anthropologist doing field work would have said anything of the sort. I was glad Dr. Scheuer wasn't there to hear.

"Of course not, ducks. Because this one is true."

"It can't be. Ghosts aren't real. Hitchhiking sailors don't vanish."

"Is that so? It seems to me, you have a few sources that think differently, don't they?"

"But there has to be an explanation!"

Trevor raised his white eyebrows again. "Does there?"

"Of course there does!" I insisted. "Dead is dead. People don't keep promises from beyond the grave. Believe me. If anyone would know that, it's me. There's an explanation."

"I thought you scientists were supposed to keep an open mind."

"Open, yes, but only to the possible."

Trevor leaned forward. "Is it so hard to believe, then, ducks?"

John Adcox

I chewed my lower lip. "Yes. Like I said. Dead is dead. Period. No miracles, no second chances. You can't beat death."

"You're sure?"

"And if you can, well . . . well why aren't there ghosts all over the place? Sam can't be the only one who died with a promise unkept."

David promised he'd come home. He said we'd have our dance. He said we'd hang our ornament, but I threw it away, and now it's gone, gone forever. . . .

"Ah. That's a question I've asked myself a few times. More than a few. Sam died during the war, when so many were dying, so many young men, and before their time . . . maybe one just slipped through the cracks. The Pearly Gates must've been wide open, don't you think? Maybe they missed one young man, a man who wanted to be home more than he wanted streets paved with gold. That's what I think, anyway. How about you, ducks?"

"I think it's impossible. Dead's dead."

"And you've examined all the evidence, then?"

"Apparently not. But there *is* an explanation."

"Then probe away, ducks. I hope you find it. Because God knows, I'd like to hear it myself. But the answers you're looking for . . . I don't think this is how you're going to find them."

I frowned. "What do you mean?"

"Turn that recorder off, just for a tick, why don't you?"

I swallowed. I nodded. I did.

128

"You've met Sam too, haven't you?"

"Me? No! Of course not."

"Ah. I thought you might have. There's a look about you. I've met some of the others, you know. We get together now and then. Kind of a support group, you might say. It's a rather exclusive club, but there's more of us than you might think. Y'see, we all share something in common. Those of us who've met Sam, I mean. We've all suffered a loss, an especially painful one." *Of course!* That was in my notes. I'd almost forgotten that detail. Trevor took a breath before he continued. "Mine was my sweet wife, may Heaven bless her soul. That true for you, too. Isn't it? Don't bother to deny it. I can see it in your eyes."

I closed my eyes and managed a nod. "Yes. God."

"So you understand. Family?"

"My husband."

"Ah," said Trevor. "Poor ducks. I'm sorry. And so young! But all of us . . . we've found, well, a strange sort of comfort, haven't we? Just to know that death isn't the end, that the soul endures. It was a gift for us. But not you. I'm right, yes?"

I nodded again. I couldn't look at him.

"Listen to me. We're not crazy. And if you ever see Sam, and I have a feeling you will, well, remember this. You're not going crazy, either."

"Unless it's an epidemic." I regretted the joke as soon as I'd spoken the words.

"Is that what you think?" Trevor asked me.

"There's an explanation."

"Is there?"

"There has to be."

"But why?"

"Because it's not possible!"

"And if I needed a scientist, that's exactly the attitude I'd want from her, sure. But when intellect fails, well, I'd want her to use her heart, wouldn't I?"

"I don't know what you mean."

Trevor looked me right in the eye as he answered. I wanted to look away, but I couldn't. "Science is for the possible. Beyond that? That's where faith comes in, isn't it? You can't hide from this, ducks, and denial's no safe harbor."

"I don't understand."

Trevor shrugged. "I don't know. Maybe I'm wrong. I've been so plenty of times before, sure. If my beloved were still with us, she'd be the first to tell you so. But something tells me you're a part of the story, now, Jessie Malone. It has a gift for you. For some reason, I don't think it's finished with you yet. Not like the rest of us. Here's the thing about stories. They're meant to be told. You of all people should know that. When we bottle them up inside, they wound us. When we tell them . . . well now, they heal us, don't they? Sam's story is your story, now. The question is, ducks, how are you going to tell it? Well?"

8

The Expectant Tenant

I almost didn't know what to think. On the one hand, I'd done it! By gum jiggity, I'd gosh-darn *done it!* I'd traced at least one variant of an urban legend back to an original source, an actual author. Not a friend of a friend, but a man who claimed to have been personally involved. I couldn't wait to call Dr. Scheuer.

Of course, I was no closer to an answer of how or why, despite Trevor's strange advice. But down deep in my heart, I was certain that was just a matter of time. As I walked back towards my flat from the tube station, I turned the puzzle over and over again in my head. Maybe, despite Jason's investigations, there was some kind of connection between Trevor Longbottom and Colm Jameson's cousin Mickey Smythe. There must be.

But that would have to mean that Mr. Longbottom had lied both to me and to Jason when he said he didn't know Colm and Mickey. I frowned. Frankly, that just didn't feel right. Call it a gut feeling, but I like to think I'm a pretty good judge of character. Mr. Longbottom didn't seem crazy, and he certainly didn't seem like a liar. Why, he'd served in Her Majesty's armed forces in India, for crying out loud. He'd looked me straight in the eye as he'd told me his story, and again when he told me it was true. More, he had nothing to gain by lying, save the risk of looking like an idiot. A part of me at least was convinced that he honestly believed that everything he'd told me was true.

But it still didn't make sense. The details Trevor Longbottom had reported matched the common details of the story that Colm and all those countless others had reported almost too precisely. Jason said he'd checked for a connection, but it was always possible he'd missed something, or that someone (everyone?) had lied. Besides, Sam's ghost was just something Jason had stumbled upon; urban legends aren't his specialty. Maybe he *had* missed something. Maybe they'd all read an account printed somewhere. I'd certainly found plenty. Maybe . . . maybe their memories were playing tricks. That was certainly possible. But like I said, Trevor Longbottom didn't seem like a liar. Colm, at least, didn't seem to know that others had reported the same story.

So I'd found an original source. But that didn't add up, either. If Mr. Longbottom had indeed invented the story, or heard it and repeated it, the model suggested that some details would shift as he revised and polished it with time—he would gradually alter subtle elements to make a better story. Heaven knows I'd interviewed enough storytellers in my academic career to know that hitherto universal tendency. And Mickey had showed absolutely no interest in telling the story at all. That didn't fit the model, either.

Sam's ghost defied logic.

I wished I could talk about the puzzle with David. I wished I could talk with him about anything.

I frowned again as I turned the key and opened the door to my flat.

Then it hit me. There was another common detail, at least in Mickey and Mr. Longbottom's accounts—one that just might be the connection I'd been looking for, even if it was a bit of a stretch. More, it might be something I could verify empirically. I didn't even bother to remove my coat, hat, and gloves as I raced to the phone, even though the latter made it hard to dial.

"Hi there," I said when Colm answered. "This is Jessie Malone. Look, I'm so sorry to bother you again—"

"Ah, Jessie, it's no trouble at all. But I'm afraid I haven't spoken to Mickey for you yet. I thought it would be easier at Christmas, like I told you, when he has a little mulled wine in him. You know. To loosen him up a little, sure."

"That sounds like a good idea," I agreed. "But listen, I was hoping maybe you could find the answer to just one question for me. Something simple."

"I'd be delighted to try, Jessie. What is it?"

"Can you find out if Mickey remembers the address where Sam asked to be taken?"

"I'll see what I can do," he promised me. "I'll call now."

He rang me back not ten minutes later with an answer. "Mickey remembers the address, sure enough," he told me. "It seems they drove to it so many times that night it's rather drilled into his head, isn't it? It's number 39 Marley Lane. Does that help you?"

"It certainly does," I assured him. A quick glance at my notes confirmed what I already knew—it was the same address Trevor Longbottom had given me.

I thanked Colm profusely. Then I buttoned my coat and left again. I had another lead to investigate. David would have been proud.

I didn't take the tube. I felt fairly confident navigating London on my own, at least with a map or a phone, but I'd never wandered as far as Hampstead and it was starting to get late. I didn't want to get lost and risk arriving too late to knock, so I sprung for a black cab. It seemed appropriate, somehow. The cabbie knew just where to go. It's the Knowledge, isn't it?

I paid my fare, got out, and found myself in front of a plain brick flat, just like Colm and Trevor had described. I took a few deep breaths. I was going to knock on the door of a total stranger. I didn't bother to collect my nerve. If

I'd stopped to do that, why, I'd still be back in my flat fretting about it. It was time to reinforce the archetype of the brash American and the politely reserved Englishman in the mind of at least one Hampstead flat tenant.

It was just about dusk when I stood on the small porch and used the brass knocker to rap on the door at number 39 Marley Lane. A man dressed in neatly pressed khaki pants and a sweater opened the door and looked at me expectantly. He puffed on a pipe; the smoke smelled faintly of cherry. "Yes?"

"Good evening, sir," I began quickly. "I'm truly sorry to bother you. I'm a cultural anthropology doctoral candidate. I wonder if I might ask you just a few questions? About..." I swallowed to compose myself before I continued. "About Sam Prescott."

The man's eyebrows lifted up towards the lock of hair that fell across his forehead, rather like twin halves of a raised drawbridge. "Sam?" he said with an amused smile. "You're a trifle early, now, aren't you?"

"So it's true." I swallowed again. "People come here. With a man called Sam—"

"Look," said the man. "I've got an article I must get finished before the morning, so I'm afraid my time is a bit short. Why don't you come in for a moment or two, tell me a little about what you're after, and perhaps we can make an appointment for after the holidays. How does that sound?"

"That sounds very generous," I said with a smile. "Thank you."

"Please come in," he said as he offered me his hand to shake. "My name is Roger Matthews, by the way."

I accepted his hand and followed him into a little parlor adjacent to his entrance foyer. We sat down on opposite sides of a little writing table. "May I get you a spot of something to drink? A sherry, perhaps? Or since you're American, perhaps a soft drink?"

"No, thank you. Really, Mr. Matthews, I don't want to take too much of your time. I feel awful enough dropping in on you like this—"

"But such is the quest for knowledge, eh? And please, call me Roger."

"Thank you, Roger. Would you mind if I record our talk?"

"Not at all."

I tapped the icon on my phone. "You say you have an article due. Are you a writer?"

"Business reporter. I freelance for the *Times* and the *Financial Times,* a few other publications of that sort. Dry stuff, really, but I like it well enough, and it keeps the lights on."

Certainly sounds like a reliable witness, I judged.

"But that's not what you came to talk about, is it?" he continued. "What can I tell you about my annual Christmas Eve visitors?"

"Do they come every year?"

"That's what annual means, isn't it?" Roger grinned.

I flushed. "I suppose it does."

"Well, for as long as I've lived here, someone's been arriving every single Christmas Eve claiming they're trying to bring a Royal Navy man called Sam Prescott home to his wife for the holiday. Every year, they go back to their car to discover that the poor bloke has disappeared without a trace. My landlady, Mrs. Jenkins, lived here for quite a few years before I moved in, and she swears the same thing used to happen to her. She actually warned me before I took the place. Said I should never expect to be in bed before midnight on Christmas Eve!"

"And it's happened every single year? Even last year?"

"Every last one, even the last. It's become something of a little holiday tradition for the missus and me, you know. We drink some hot chocolate or maybe a little port, wrap the last of our gifts, and read or watch an old movie on the television. When Sam comes, why, we know it's time to pop off to bed."

"What happens?"

"Oh, I'm sure you must know, or you wouldn't be here, would you?"

"Would you mind telling me yourself?"

"There's not all that much to it, really," said Roger. "'Round midnight, some frazzled and hapless bloke shows up saying he's got a Navy man called Sam Prescott waiting in the car, a man who's desperate to get home to his wife for Christmas."

"Always a man?"

"So far."

"What do you know about her? The wife, I mean."

"Not much," he confessed. "Just the name, really. Emily. Once or twice I even got a middle name, or rather a maiden name. Wilson."

"What else?"

"That's about it, really." Roger took another puff on his pipe and watched the silver smoke drift away. "They show up wanting to know if we can help find this chap's home, and when they look, *poof!* He's disappeared without a trace. I've no idea how; as you can see, the street's pretty empty. I doubt he'd even have time to run to the next house, would he? Not without me seeing him. And believe me, I always look. The year we had the snow, why, he didn't even leave any footprints."

I took a deep breath. "So how do you explain it?"

Roger chuckled again. "I'm not sure I can. Though God and all the saints know I've tried. I used to think it was some kind of serial practical joke, you know. I thought if I waited long enough, they'd come 'round to the punch line at last. But in all the years, that's never happened. And the people who show up, well . . . they all seem so earnest, so sincere. And so genuinely puzzled and, yes, even distraught when Sam pulls his little disappearing act."

"So you believe them?"

"Well, I don't know about that," Roger said, sending another puff of smoke drifting towards the ceiling. "But I suppose I believe they all believe what they're saying." *Just what I'd thought about Mr. Longbottom.* "I mean, they're quite convincing, don't you know. I rather doubt you could find that many brilliant actors if you emptied out the entire West End, would you?"

"But you must have some guess, surely," I suggested.

Roger smiled. "Maybe it is a ghost." His tone was light so I couldn't tell whether he was joking or serious. "Isn't Christmas supposed to be a time of miracles and wonders, that sort of thing? Mostly, though, my wife and I just accept it as an odd little holiday tradition. If nothing else, it gives us a good story to tell, don't you think?"

"I see."

"Now then, if you'll excuse me, I really must get back to work. I'll get you a card. Why don't you ring me after the holidays if you have more questions?"

"I will. Roger, thank you for your time. I'm so sorry to have disturbed you."

I chewed my lower lip as I left him, troubled by more questions than answers. Minding the gap, I caught the tube back toward my flat.

9

The Bewildered Graduate Student

called Jason and told him everything that had happened. He was packing, but he listened attentively all the same. Unfortunately, he had no ideas to offer—just a question. "What do you think it is?"

"Uh, think what is?"

"The gift! The one Mr. Longbottom said the story held for you?"

"Ha!" I said. "Just a bunch of frustration. Some gift, huh?"

"I don't know. I think he might be right about stories. I mean, about what they do. Maybe there's comfort for you, too. And healing. I hope so, Jess. I truly do."

"I don't need comfort, Jason. I need answers."

"Then I hope you find them. Jess?"

"Yeah?"

"I'm worried about you, pal."

"I'll be fine, Jason. Really."

"If you say so." He didn't sound especially convinced, but we hung up soon after that. I changed into my pajamas, cleaned my teeth, and popped off to bed. I needn't have bothered. I tossed and turned all night. Sam's ghost troubled my thoughts and kept sleep at bay. It just didn't make sense! Granted, I hadn't even begun to do adequate research—in-depth interviews and follow-ups to begin with, not to mention the arduous task of confirming that there were no possible links or connections between my various sources.

Could they have all seen some common published report? No, again, that would mean they were all liars, Colm and his cousin Mickey (or Mickey's mum, anyway), Mr. Longbottom, and even Roger. Somehow, I just couldn't bring myself to believe that.

Sleep didn't come. Warm milk, two glasses of wine, a hot bath, and even an allergy tablet didn't help. I was fresh out of elephant tranquilizers, so I tossed and turned until my thoughts were a jumble.

Could it really be some kind of practical joke? Had someone been intentionally fooling people every year on Christmas Eve? For more than sixty years?

No way. That would be way too weird, even for British humor.

Of course, there was one other possibility, too. The scientist in me hated myself for even thinking it, but once the idea occurred to me, I couldn't let it go. I was still thinking about it when the sun came up again.

Jessie, you are absolutely and completely insane, I chided myself as I climbed out of bed.

This is completely nuts, I thought as I cleaned my teeth and dressed. *Dead is dead. People don't keep promises from beyond the grave. They can't!*

You're an idiot, Malone, I told the tired face in the mirror. Bloodshot eyes above puffy dark circles stared back at me.

You're a crazy fool and you're wasting your time, I scolded myself as I locked my door and left.

It took me three stops to find the information I was looking for, but find it I did. Say this for the British—they are amazingly efficient record keepers.

There really had been a British Naval Officer called Sam Prescott, a midshipman. He died in the North Sea off the coast of Germany on December 23, 1943. He was survived by a wife, Emily Wilson Prescott. They'd been married less than seven months.

That doesn't mean anything, I reminded myself. *So what if there's a Sam Prescott? One that just happened to die close to the point where the reports of Sam's ghost first appeared? If this whole thing was an elaborate hoax or a*

practical joke, anyone could have heard or found the name of an actual sailor.

But why on Earth would they?

Nothing made sense. That phrase was becoming a mantra for me.

Here was a tale that defied all models of how urban legends were supposed to originate and spread. If the central character hadn't been a ghost, I'd have been convinced that I'd stumbled upon a true account, an actual event that had inspired a new urban myth.

But it did involve a ghost. And that was impossible, wasn't it?

Wasn't it?

Of course it was. Dead is dead. I of all people knew that all too bloody well.

I don't believe in ghosts. I'm a scientist, dammit. Somebody's playing a trick.

Even though the rational part of me knew better, I couldn't let go of the question. In any case, I knew I had to find out more. Once again, those excellent British public record keepers had valuable information for me, even if they were rather less than completely focused on the last business day before Christmas Eve.

Roger's flat had been built in 1962. A house on the same plot had stood for nearly a century before it was damaged in a fire. It didn't take much work to find a list of owners of the property—it was, after all, a matter of public record. A Sam and Emily Prescott were listed as the owners from June, 1943 to February, 1944. Emily alone had signed the deed when the property was sold.

Poor Emily, I thought. *A war widow, far from home.* I wondered what happened to her.

More puzzled than ever, I went home.

I don't believe in ghosts. Scientists don't accept the impossible.

But what happens when the impossible is the only explanation left?

Oh, David. David. Why didn't you come home to me? Why can't I say goodbye to you?

Back at my flat, I brewed a pot of herbal tea, even though I wanted coffee, and booted up my computer. I'd planned to write up my notes, but instead I found myself launching my Internet browser. Even before I realized what I was doing, I called up an American national directory site, and typed in the name Emily Prescott. It was silly; I knew that. I had no idea if Emily had returned home to America after her husband's death, or if she'd remarried, or even if she still lived. Even if I found her, what then? I'd have no way to know if I'd found the same Emily. I certainly couldn't just call her up out of the blue. Could I?

My heart skipped a beat. My search found thirty-six Emily Prescotts in the United States—but only two Emily W. Prescotts, one in Portland, one in Atlanta.

I didn't bother to do the math; it was barely evening here in London so it would be more or less midday in

America. Before I was even fully aware of what I was doing, I found myself reaching for the phone. I dialed the Portland number first.

What the hell am I doing? She's surely remarried, or dead, or. . . .

"Hello?" An older woman's voice.

"Hi," I said. "May I speak to Emily Prescott please?"

"I'm sorry," the woman replied. "Emily's not home from school yet. She called from the road; we're expecting her in about an hour or so. Can I have her call you back?" Uh oh. This Emily was apparently a university student! Obviously, she couldn't have married Sam in 1943.

"No thank you," I said. Then, embarrassed, I hung up before she could question me further.

What in the world am I even doing?

I poured a fresh cup of tea, drank it in a gulp, and poured another. I knew I'd never be able to rest until I called the final Emily W., so I took a deep breath for courage. Then I dialed quickly before I could change my mind. A young-sounding man answered on the fourth ring.

"Hi," I said. "Um . . . may I speak to Emily, please?"

He hesitated for a second before he answered. "May I ask who's calling, please?"

"Uh, yeah, my name is Jessie Malone," I answered. "I'm. . . ." Oh God. What was I going to say? "I'm a graduate student working on a fellowship in London. I've been researching a British sailor named Sam Prescott. I'm trying to locate an American woman named Emily that married him. Do you know if I have the right Emily?"

The man laughed, a warm and happy sound. "That she is, and I wish she was here. She loves to talk about her Sam, even to perfect strangers when she can find one that'll listen!"

"Forgive me for being rude, but may I ask to whom I'm speaking?"

"Oh, sure. My name's Jim Wilson. She's my aunt."

"Nice to meet you, Jim."

"Pleasure. Is there anything else I can help you with? This is kind of a bad time, I'm afraid."

"Are you expecting her soon?"

"God, I hope so," he said. "But . . . I'm afraid not. She's down at Piedmont Hospital. Her heart. It, um . . . well, at her age. . . ." His voice broke a little. "I'm not sure how good she's doing."

"Oh, I'm so sorry!"

"I appreciate that. I wish she could talk to you. God! She'd be thrilled to hear that someone wanted to ask about her Sam, and all the way from London, too! Are you doing some kind of World War II history thing? She was a nurse, you know."

"I didn't," I said, glad to have a convenient way to avoid his first question. Let him assume what he would. "She went home to the States after Sam died?"

"She did. She always said she couldn't bear to stay in the little house where she'd waited for him to come home, not when she knew he'd never arrive." *That I can understand.*

Jim must be close to his aunt, I guessed. He seemed to like to talk about her. Maybe he found it comforting. I told myself I was helping as much as prying and I almost believed it.

"And she never remarried?"

"She never did. She never stopped loving her Sam. If . . . if the worst happens, we're all going to miss her something awful. And that's going to happen very soon, I'm afraid. But in a way, I'm almost happy for her, too. You see, in all those years, she never stopped missing him. I'm glad they'll be together at last. Sam died at Christmas, too. Did you know that?"

"I did," I said softly.

"He died on the very day before he was to begin his leave," Jim said. "He promised her he'd be home for Christmas, but he never made it."

Not yet, I thought. *But apparently, he's been trying ever since. But she went home to America. He doesn't know where to find her.*

No, no. Stop that. It's impossible. Dead is dead. Like David.

"Families should be together for Christmas," I said, thinking of my father, and thinking of David.

"That's true," said Jim. "Poor Aunt Emily. She said she never felt like she was home for Christmas, because she was never with the man she loved. 'Home's where Sam is,' she used to say, 'and there I never go.'"

I swallowed and hoped Jim couldn't hear. "That's so sad."

"I wish I could have known him. Anybody who can inspire that much love must have been a very special man."

"He must have. And . . . I have a feeling he never stopped loving her, either."

"That's nice to hear. Listen, why don't I take your number? Maybe. . . ." His voice broke a bit again. "Maybe she'll feel well enough to call you. I'd at least like to tell her you phoned. It'll cheer her, I think."

I gave him my information, wished him a Happy Christmas, and hung up.

I honestly didn't know what to do after that. I looked back over my notes, but I couldn't make myself read them. The tears kept getting in the way. Eventually, I left my work there on the table, put on my coat, and went out. I must have walked for an hour at least, maybe two. I stopped by a pub and ordered a sandwich and a salad, but I hardly ate a bite. I walked some more. I thought about Sam; I thought about David. Mostly, I thought about poor Emily Wilson Prescott, another

149

lonely bride, waiting alone on Christmas Eve for a husband who would never come.

I found Jason waiting for me in my kitchen when I finally made it back home.

"Hey there," he said. That's when I noticed he had his suitcases with him. He'd stopped by on his way to the airport. He was leaving. Right, of course he was leaving. He was going home for Christmas. But he'd come by to see me first, and that made me smile.

"Jason! What are you doing here?"

"Good to see you, too." He grinned and shrugged. "I can't stay long. I just wanted to check on you before I head off. David . . . David would have wanted me to."

I nodded. David would have certainly wanted that. Jason was sitting at the table where I'd been doing my work. "You've been reading my notes," I accused.

He nodded and shrugged again, but otherwise ignored the question. "It's good reading."

"Uh . . . thanks?"

"You're welcome. You should come with me, you know. To the airport, I mean. I bet you can still get a ticket to Alabama. Or Atlanta, anyway. Even though you'll probably be stuck in a middle seat."

"I can't. I told you that."

"Why? And don't play the work card; I already know you got an extension from Dr. Scheuer. You told me."

I had to look away. "I can't. No. I . . . I'm not ready, Jason. I'm not." I took a breath and tried to change the subject. "You should hurry. Holiday traffic—"

"Sit down," said Jason. "There's time."

I sat.

"Now then. Want to tell me what's going on?"

"Jason—"

Jason held up a hand to stop me. "Jessie, please. You haven't been yourself in . . . God, I can't even remember how long. I know it's been hard. I mean, David . . . my God, I don't know how you do it. I don't know how you even get out of bed in the morning."

And just then, I was starting to cry. "I don't always," I admitted. "I'm a mess, Jason. I shouldn't be around people. Not even you. I think . . . I think maybe I'm falling apart."

"That's okay. I mean, tacos fall apart, right? And we still love them. But there's something else. Isn't there." It wasn't really a question.

I looked away and wiped my eyes on my sleeve. "I don't know what you mean."

"Jessie. Please. I've been reading your notes, yo."

"Maybe . . . maybe I really am cracking up."

"Is that what you think?"

"I don't know what to think any more, Jason. I don't!"

"You're starting to believe. In Sam's ghost, I mean. Aren't you?"

And dammit, I was crying again. "I . . . I don't know, Jason. Nothing makes sense anymore. Not one bloody stupid thing!"

"Jessie, why didn't you tell me?"

"I did. I told you most."

"You didn't tell me all. You didn't tell me that you'd checked Sam's records, the house. . . ."

"No."

"Why not?"

"Well, I just did a lot of it."

"And?"

"Because I'm supposed to be a goddamn woman of science, Jason. Not . . . not the chick from the *X-men.*"

"X-files," Jason corrected me. To my credit, I didn't slap him.

"And I'm not crazy. I'm not, Jason!"

"Of course not. But Jessie, you have to talk about this."

I turned back and hit him full on with my best glare, which I'm pretty sure was effective even through the tears, because I saw him flinch. "I don't have to do anything."

"Jessie. You know what this means. Don't you?"

I left the kitchen and dropped down on my sofa. "It means I am crazy. Crackers. I'm falling apart."

Jason followed and pulled the chair close. "It doesn't have to mean that."

"Yes, Jason. Yes it does. Dead is dead. Believe me. I of all people would know that. So what else can it mean? Well? Huh?"

"Maybe . . . and I'm not quite a scientist yet, but . . . maybe it means you found a miracle, Jessie."

I closed my eyes again. "There's no such thing."

"Sure there is. That's kind of the point of the present season, isn't it?"

"That's what David used to say."

"He was a smart dude."

"Yeah? Well, what about my miracle? Huh? Where were all the damn miracles when David died? We never hung our ornament, Jason. We . . . we never had our first dance!"

"So hang the ornament now."

"I can't. I threw it away. I threw it away because I'm stupid and hurting and because there's no such thing as goddamn miracles."

"I think there is," Jason said.

"Then where the hell is mine?" I demanded. "Well?"

Jason took a deep breath before he answered. "Maybe all the days he was alive, all the time you had together . . . maybe that was your miracle. Or maybe . . . maybe this is your miracle. Maybe the story holds a miracle for you, just like Mr. Longbottom said."

"I don't know what you're talking about."

"Or maybe, maybe . . . I don't know. Or maybe . . . maybe this is your chance to be someone else's miracle. And yeah, a miracle for love. But someone else's love."

"No. No. That doesn't count."

"Of course it does," said Jason. "Nothing that we do for love is ever lost."

"No. No." I shook my head. "That's not fair. It's not!"

"Maybe it's Emily you can help. She's sick, right? Although I guess she can't love a dead man."

"Like hell. I love a dead man. Yeah. I kept right on loving David, and he's dead! He died! He left me, Jason. He left me, and I still can't let him go! You . . . you don't even know what it's like, do you?"

"What?" said Jason.

"Do you know what it's like to lose the person you love? Do you? Do you? No? Let me tell you something, Jason. Here's what's amazing about love. It really is every bit as great as you think it's going to be." And then the tears came in earnest, and I couldn't stop them. "Do you know what it's like, Jason? Well? Can you imagine what it's like to have it fill you with so much light that you feel like you've swallowed the sun? And then to have it all just . . . just snatched away. . . . Can you imagine that? Can you? Can you even imagine how God damn unfair that is?"

Jason sighed and shook his head. "Oh, Christ. No. No it isn't."

I blinked. "W—what?"

"I don't think it's unfair. You're right. Jessie. I can't imagine it. Know why? It's because most of us never even get a stupid chance, to find what you had, not even once. Do you know what I'd give to feel that way? And . . . and oh my God! To have someone feel that way in return? Do you have any idea what I'd give, what I'd risk for that? Even if I knew all the agony that's sure as hell gonna follow? Because the agony, Jessie . . . that's part of the deal. That's life. Yeah. That's being alive. And it's a hell of a lot better than feeling nothing. Believe me. Do you know what I'd give to feel that way? For just one stupid minute? So no, Jessie. I don't think it's unfair. I don't think it's unfair at all."

I blinked again. I had no idea how to answer him.

I didn't sleep much that night, either, although I think I slipped in and out of a light, dozing dream state. Even then, my mind still wrestled with the paradigm-defying story of Sam's ghost, and the fact of his very real wife, apparently living out her last hours in a hospital a continent away.

My scientist's mind considered a thousand theories and dismissed them all, one by one, until, deep in the night, the only possibility left to me was the impossible one. I struggled with that a bit, but the logical part of my brain was too sleepy to put up much of a fight.

That's probably why so many miracles seem to be accomplished in darkness.

I've been slowly preparing myself for this, I realized then. *In Paris, in Germany, in the chippy with Trevor Longbottom. Even when I argued with Jason. Ever since I first heard the tale from Colm in the pub.*

Somehow, the lonely ghost of Sam Prescott wandered the earth once a year, desperate to get home to his wife because he'd made a promise. I don't know why his restless spirit didn't find rest and peace in Heaven, as I'd been taught in Sunday School as a girl. Or maybe I did. For Sam, Heaven wasn't a place of clouds and harps and golden light; it was a pretty American girl. Heaven was where Emily was. It couldn't be paradise without her, not for him. She was his home, and he hers. Love called to him, like a star in a cold, dark sky on Christmas Eve. I knew that in the deepest and truest part of my heart.

Perhaps it was the lack of sleep, or perhaps my thoughts were dusted with the glittering stuff of dreams, but somewhere in the night doubt faded away. By morning, I'd reached a decision.

Sam and Emily needed a miracle. I hadn't gotten one, but maybe Jason was right. Maybe I could be one instead.

10

The Appearing Hitchhiker

It was close to noon on Christmas Eve. I'd hired a car and found my way down to Clink Street on the other side of the Thames. I had no idea at all what I expected to find, but I knew I had to go there. If it turned out to be some hoaxer or a practical joker, well, he'd *wish* he was a ghost by the time I got through with him. Although of course I didn't really believe that. In the deepest part of my soul, I believed I'd find Sam. He'd made a promise. Emily was waiting. I had to get him home for Christmas.

I had to.

I tried to think of what Colm and Mr. Longbottom had told me, as well as what I'd read in the other accounts. They had all experienced some personal loss. That I had in spades. Had they done anything else that might be special? Anything that might make Sam choose them? I tried to think back over my notes. Mickey had been drinking; could that have something to do with it? Did alcohol open one's senses to the next world? But no, Mr. Longbottom had been driving his cab. He surely wouldn't have had a drink. He'd told me as much. Try as I might, I couldn't think of anything else. Which is a good thing, I expect. It's hard enough to drive in London stone sober when all one has to do is worry about the traffic, the rain and the fog, and driving on the wrong bloody side of the road.

All the same, I wished for a good stiff drink. One needs fortification when hunting ghosts—spirits for a spirit, so to speak.

I circled the neighborhood around Clink Street and the ruins of Winchester House a dozen times and more. I passed the street where David and I had taken our dance lessons, where he'd wanted to learn disco. I passed The Admiral's Men Pub and wondered idly if Mickey and his mates were huddled inside, raising a pint to old times. I wondered if they all still came, to renew their love and share old times, and to remember their late friend. I hoped so. Traditions should endure.

I drove, I circled, I explored. I didn't see a single hitchhiker.

I didn't stop looking, though. I told the protesting scientist inside me to sit down and shut up. When dawn arrived on Christmas Eve morning, I found that logic had fled, and the bright and golden light of pure faith was born. Faith in what? I'm not sure I can say, to be honest. Faith in Christmas, faith in miracles, and faith in love that transcends death. All of that and more. I knew in my heart that if I kept looking, I'd find Sam Prescott. Not David, no, David was gone, just like our First Married Christmas ornament, the one I'd never hang. But I would find Sam. And when I did, I'd find a way to get him home to his Emily. Before it was too late.

But I had to find him soon; we had a long way to travel before Christmas Day. I'd booked two tickets on a flight to Atlanta. Luck was with me; the flight was nearly empty. I'd find some way to pay the credit card bill later. I had no idea how I'd get Sam onto a plane with a 60-year-old passport (assuming ghosts even carry ID at all) but I figured if he could beat the grave, airport security shouldn't prove too much of a challenge.

Have faith, I told myself. *Have faith.* That's what David would have wanted.

Sam always disappeared around midnight, but I had to hope that meant local time. It was an eight-hour flight, give or take, but we'd gain five hours thanks to the time zones. If he stayed on London time, well, he'd disappear somewhere over the Atlantic and it would all be for nothing. Surely fate wouldn't be that cruel. Not now, not now that I was here to help him. We'd arrive around dusk, Atlanta time, if all went well. That should give us a few hours to get to the hospital, find her room, and find some way in. I had no idea how ghostly apparitions

159

worked or what unearthly rules they followed, so I had to hope for the best.

Faith, I reminded myself again. *Faith.*

It was just after one in the afternoon when I found him.

It was raining much harder then and the figure in front of me seemed almost to appear out of nowhere. No ghostly powers were responsible for that; at least I don't think so. I was paying too much attention to a steering wheel on the wrong side of the stupid car and trying to find a turn in that pervasive English mist—and not nearly enough to potential obstacles in the road in front of me.

I slammed on my brakes, but even so I nearly hit the man.

All the same, in that instant when the lurch of adrenaline gave way to a flush of relief, I smiled. The man in front of me had been trying to wave me down. He was hitchhiking, and from the frantic expression on his face, he seemed to be in a desperate hurry. He wore a blue Navy uniform. *Idiot.* I gave myself a mental smack on the forehead. *You never researched the uniform.* I had no idea whether the blues he wore were modern or decades out of date. It's funny the things you think about.

My heart was thumping, and my hands were sweating so much that I had trouble gripping the handle as I rolled down my window. "Hi there," I said. "Looks like you could use a ride."

The man grinned, and I was shocked by how boyish he looked. "Oh, thank you! Yes, thank you, please!"

He ran around and climbed in. He smelled faintly (but not unpleasantly) of damp wool and something mustier, like freshly tilled earth in a garden. The car seemed suddenly colder as he slammed his door shut.

It was he; I knew it without a shade of doubt. The uniform, the location, Christmas Eve. All the same, my blood turned to frost in my veins when he spoke. "Thanks again, Ma'am. I can't tell you how much I appreciate your help. My name's Sam Prescott, by the way."

Oh my God. Oh my God. Oh. . . .

My throat tightened and I couldn't make my voice work. All of London must have heard the cannon thunder sound of my heart pounding in my chest, loud as the Nazi bombing during World War II.

"Um . . . are you okay, Miss?"

"S . . . sorry," I managed to squeak at last. *I must look like I've seen a ghost*, I thought. The old joke didn't comfort me, although I wished I could share it. I swallowed before I continued. "I . . . couldn't talk for a second there."

"I don't blame you," he said politely. "What with me jumping out at you like that. But I've been trying all day to get some help. It's like people just drive right on by without even seeing me!"

Pull yourself together, Jessie, I commanded myself. This is what you wanted, dammit. This is the answer. . . .

I couldn't reply. Words failed me again. I didn't even drive—I simply stared at the young man sitting next to me. He didn't *look* like a ghost. Would a spook smell of soil and wool? Of anything? I shuddered.

"I really need a ride, if there's any way at all you can spare the time." I liked his voice, with its youthful, earnest vitality and obvious enthusiasm.

That's it, Jess. Concentrate on his voice, yes, his words. Anything. . . .

"I've got to get home, Miss," he said when I didn't respond. "It's important." I still didn't answer. "I need to get up to Hampstead. Please. I know it's probably out of your way. . . ."

A car behind me pounded his horn and, startled into action, I started the car moving. "Why Hampstead?" I asked when I found my voice at last. I knew the answer, but I needed to hear the words; I needed to hear him say it. I had to be sure.

"My wife's there." I heard the smile in his voice as he gushed. "Emily. She's American, like you, and pretty as a peach. You should come in and meet her. We haven't been married all that long, but I promised her. I promised her I'd be home for Christmas. And look, here I am, sure as you please!"

Oh my God.

"Sam," I said, proud of how well I kept the quiver out of my voice. "You've been trying to get home for a long time, haven't you?"

"I don't . . . I. . . ." Suddenly, the bright voice seemed uncertain, even confused. "I just have to get home. For Christmas," he finished firmly, as though troubled by where his thoughts were leading him. "It's number 39 Marley Lane."

I turned back towards the river. I'd memorized the directions to the airport—God knows how he'd react to an iPhone and GPS—but in the tense emotion of the moment, I'd gotten myself rather flustered. I couldn't quite get my bearings. And my mind was awhirl with questions for my passenger.

"How long were you trying to get a ride, Sam?"

"Oh, all night, Miss! And all day, too, if you can believe it. Must have been since around midnight. People, they just didn't even seem to see me! Like I wasn't even there. Until you, that is."

So he'd been around since midnight, the very first moment of Christmas Eve. But people couldn't see him. So why? Maybe it took an act of will for him to make people see him. Maybe he'd been trying all night, just like he did every year, but it took him a while to pull it off.

Of course it takes an act of will, I thought. *Like the ultimate act of will required to keep a promise to his beloved, even from beyond the grave.*

Thinking back over the earliest accounts I'd read back in France and Germany, Sam used to appear as early as two a.m. or so. But lately, at least in Mickey and Trevor Longbottom's accounts, it was later in the day—more like three or four in the afternoon at the earliest. Maybe it was getting harder for him to manifest with every passing Christmas. I'd bucked the trend a little, but then, I'd been looking for him. Maybe that made a difference. Such was the best hypothesis I could formulate. But who knows? I could have been way off base. Maybe people were just too busy to notice the plight of their fellow man at Christmas.

I wished I had some definitive manual on spectral apparitions. I wished I knew how phantoms worked, or what supernatural metaphysics governed them. I didn't, though, so I'd have to do the best I could.

"This isn't the first time you've tried to get home, is it, Sam?"

"I don't understand," he said hesitantly.

"I think you've been trying to get home for a very long time, haven't you?"

"I . . . I don't know . . . I. . . ."

"What's the last thing you remember?"

"I . . . I don't know," he said, and I heard something awful, something melding hurt and desperation into a terrible alloy of emotion, in his voice. As he spoke, the last of my fear melted to compassion, the way shadows are transformed by light. "It . . . it's like a dream. I keep trying to get home to Emily, Miss, but I can't . . . I can't find her. . . ."

"I know," I told him as gently as I could. "I know, Sam. It happens every year, doesn't it? You try to get home, but you can't. And then you're trying again, but it's harder, isn't it? And the city looks different, subtly but relentlessly changed. Doesn't it?"

"I . . . I don't know. I think . . . I don't know London all that well, Miss. Maybe I'm just lost. Yes. That's it. Especially with all this rain and fog. If you can kindly just help me get my bearings a bit—"

Thank God it's London; old cities change more slowly. America, where we erase our cities like blackboards and sweep our history away to make room for the new, would have driven him nuts.

I took a deep breath. "Sam," I began, "I know why you can't get home. I know why you can't find Emily."

"Please," he said, and the ache in his voice tore at my heart. "Please help me."

"Emily's not here," I told him. "She. . . ." *Oh God, how do I word this? How do I tell him that he died years—no, decades—ago?* "She didn't know you were coming, Sam."

"No," he said firmly. "No, that can't be."

"She went home, Sam. Home to America."

"No!"

"I can take you there, Sam. I can take you to her. If you want me to."

"Please," he said. "Please. I promised her."

"I'll get you home to her, Sam. For Christmas. I promise."

11

The Original Source

We arrived at Gatwick Airport with an hour and a half to spare. That should give us just enough time to pass security and reach the gate in time for the final boarding call, if barely, since I didn't have luggage to check. I could carry on my single bag and Sam would just have to do the same with his phantom duffle. It was a little closer than I like to cut things at the airport, especially for an international flight, but as long as we hurried, we'd be okay. Or so I hoped. After all, David and I had done even worse after our wedding, and we'd made it.

Next came the hard part. I had tickets and I had Sam. But these days, security was tighter than ever—not that it mattered; I wouldn't have known how to slip him past even the most incompetent security in the most relaxed airport on the planet. I had no idea how I'd get Sam through to the gate, much less onto the plane.

Wait, I thought then. *It takes an act of will. He has to make people see him.* Or so I'd deduced. Once again, I remembered that I had no idea how ghostly manifestations actually worked. I could only pray that my guess was right.

"Sam, listen to me," I whispered urgently as we hurried from the car park to the terminal. His eyes were wide as he watched the jumbo jets taking off. I spoke a little louder to be sure I had his attention. "It took a long time for you to make people see you, didn't it?"

I hated myself for asking him that. I knew I was making him confront things he didn't want to face; I was making him accept what he was, what had happened to him. I hated myself, but I had no choice.

"You had to concentrate, Sam. Am I right?"

He didn't speak. He simply nodded uneasily, once, without looking at me.

"This is important. Can you . . . can you maybe not concentrate on being seen for a little while? We have to get on a plane, Sam. An airplane. It's the only way to get you home to Emily. But you . . . you don't have the paperwork you need. Do you understand me?"

He nodded again.

"Just stay with me. Stay real close and follow me. But Sam, please. Please don't let them see you, okay? It's important. Once we take off, it'll be just fine. I bought you a ticket, so you'll have an empty seat to sit in. Okay, Sam?"

"Okay," he echoed softly.

We hurried across the drive towards the terminal entrance. I looked back, and saw Sam hurrying after.

Damn! If Sam was trying to make himself invisible, it wasn't working. His mouth hung open as he took in all the sights around him. I guided him through an alien world. He didn't disappear.

My pulse quickened again, this time with fear rather than excitement. I reminded myself to have faith, but anxiety proved stronger.

There was a short line at the check-in counter, and I hurried that way. I made a point of not looking back at Sam; like a child, I hoped that if I didn't see him, maybe nobody else would either.

Please, oh please!

My heartbeat thundered as I reached the counter, and once again my palms were sweating so profusely that I nearly dropped my ID and passport.

The agent confirmed that I'd packed my own bags and kept track of them, then handed me my boarding pass. "Are you traveling alone? I see that you purchased two tickets—"

"The other's for an acquaintance," I said. I looked back. Sam was gone. "He's . . . he's traveling on his own."

"Well, he'd better hurry along, then. He'll miss the flight."

I shrugged. "He can take care of himself," I said, hoping it was true. What would he make of a modern airport, half a century after he'd last seen one? I prayed that he'd stay close; I knew he'd never find his way on his own. To him, Gatwick was the bloody Jetsons. He needed me. As I rushed away, I caught, briefly and subtly, the scent of earth and damp wool.

"Sam," I whispered urgently as I reached the moving sidewalk that would take me to the gate. "Are you there? Sam?" There was no answer, just a man looking at me rather strangely as he passed. I flushed and glanced away.

"Sam?" I whispered again. No answer, only a chill that made me shiver.

I passed the spot where, a lifetime ago, I'd nearly lost the First Married Christmas ornament, and I had to choke down a fresh storm of tears.

I checked in at the gate and had just enough time to drink a pint of cider and buy a couple of good bottles of wine for Mom and Dad at the duty-free shop before it was time to board. Sam wasn't the only one with someplace to be for the holiday. Once I got him to his Emily, I could surprise my family. David would have wanted that. And maybe . . . maybe it was time. *Looks like I'll be home for Christmas after all, Daddy.* I smiled a little as the clerk rang up my purchase.

I saw no sign of Sam. I could only hope that, invisibly, he followed close to me.

Please. . . .

I boarded and folded myself into my tiny aisle seat, leaving the window for Sam. He didn't appear. I had a

bulkhead seat in Comfort Plus, the last row before business class, so I had a good view of the door. I waited.

Sam didn't come.

I waited some more, and my anxiety swelled to panic. The flight was still barely half-full, but the flow of
people slowed to a trickle.

The last of the passengers came, but still no Sam.

In the distance, I heard the gate agent make the final boarding call. No Sam.

Where could he be? Maybe he'd gotten lost. Or
maybe he'd vanished back to wherever he came from
when he stopped concentrating on being seen. Maybe
he couldn't bring himself back again.

Oh, no, no . . . please, not after all this.

The jet's massive door slammed shut with all the fi-
nality of a clap of thunder on Judgment Day. The seat
next to me remained empty.

Just a few more minutes. . . .

We started taxiing away from the gate almost immediately. The one stupid time in my entire life a flight
I was on left on time, and it was the one time I wanted
a delay.

Please. . . .

Although in my heart I knew it wouldn't matter. A
few minutes or an hour, it wouldn't matter at all.

I had failed.

Sam had counted on me and I'd failed him. Now his
Emily was breathing her last in a lonely hospital room

half a world away, and Sam would never make it to her. He'd never keep his promise. There was no such thing as miracles.

What would happen to him? Would he keep trying every Christmas Eve, year after lonesome year, even though she was gone? I didn't know. I only knew that I'd failed. I'd done the best I could, but it wasn't enough. I hadn't known what to do.

I was the only person who could have helped him, and I'd failed.

Maybe it's better this way. The Emily he remembers is young and vibrant and beautiful. Maybe it's better that he won't see her as she is now, old and dying.

But even as I thought that, I knew better. Sam loved her, his Emily, and he'd made a promise.

I'd failed him. Just like I'd failed David when I hadn't insisted he not drive that night.

We'd never hang our First Married Christmas ornament. We'd never have our stupid First Annual Alabama Christmas Hoedown and Hootenanny.

I buried my face in my hands as we reached the runway. There was no one around me, and I felt cold and alone. I was sobbing as we took off. Trying to do it quietly so that I wouldn't draw attention to myself only made it worse. I cried until the last of my tears had drained away. Then the weight of misery and two nights without rest caught up with me, and I slept.

A scent stirred me from the cold depth of sad dreams, the odor of wool, wool and something else, something dark and rich. The flight attendant whispered when she came by with the beverage cart, not wanting to wake me if I was dozing, but her voice was enough to bring me fully back to consciousness.

"Would you like anything?" she asked me.

"No thanks," I replied with a voice still thick with sleep. "Oh. Maybe a blanket?"

"They're in the overhead compartment a couple of rows back. I'll get you one in a moment."

"I'd appreciate that."

She nodded.

Then she looked to my left.

"And how about you, sir?"

I sat bolt upright and spun around.

There was Sam, sitting comfortably in the seat next to me, still dressed in his Navy blues.

"No thank you," he said softly. "I'm just fine for now." He looked at me and smiled. There was a twinkle in his blue eyes.

"Sam!" I whispered as the flight attendant wheeled her cart away. "Sam, thank God! I thought . . . I thought I'd lost you." I had to wipe away tears.

His smile widened. "I'll never be lost again. God sent me a miracle to guide me home."

I knew what he meant, but I shifted uncomfortably. "Not much of a miracle, I'm afraid."

"Enough," he replied confidently. "I made a promise, a promise to Emily, and He sent you to help me keep it."

I laughed and looked away. "I think if God wanted a miracle, He could do better than me. Red Sea, pillars of fire in the desert, stones to bread, stars in the east. That kind of thing."

Sam chuckled. "People are the greatest miracles of all. How else should God do His work?"

I flushed and turned away. In the companionable quiet, something else worried me. After a long moment, I spoke again. "Sam. I . . . I want you to be prepared. Emily . . . she's going to be different when you see her. Different from what you remember."

"I know. I think . . . I don't know. I guess I've always known that. But Miss, it's Emily I love, whether she's in an old body or not. She's still Emily. She'll always be Emily, my love."

"I'm glad, Sam."

"And besides, do you really think somebody who's been through what I've been through wouldn't know the difference between a soul and the shell? Between dust and light? Love lasts forever, ma'am, but it's a thing of the spirit, not the body."

I wanted to ask him more about that, about how he'd returned, about what death was like. I wanted to ask if he knew David. I didn't, though. Miracles aren't about answers. Besides, the flight attendant returned with my blanket and pillow before I could even articulate the questions. For the first time in my life, I let them go. I tried to hide a yawn as Sam helped me tuck myself in. He smiled again. "You go ahead and sleep. I'll be just fine."

"What about you?"

He shook his head. "I don't need too much sleep, Miss. I . . . I want to enjoy this time, you know? I want to spend it breathing, listening to you sleep, looking out at the sea and the clouds. I want to treasure it while I can."

"I understand," I said softly. I squirmed around under my blanket and adjusted my pillow to make myself as comfortable as possible. I yawned again.

I saw Sam looking at me before I closed my eyes. "Can I ask you one question before you rest?"

"Sure," I replied.

"How did you know?"

"Excuse me?"

"About . . . about me," he clarified. "How did you know to find me?"

I thought for a moment before I answered. Should I sugarcoat or try to soften the truth a bit? *No*, I decided. *He wants to know; he needs to know.* Deciding I couldn't go wrong with the truth, I told him everything—Jason and Colm in the pub, the libraries in Paris and Germany, Trevor and Roger. I told him everything except, for some reason, about David. This was for him, him and Emily, not me. It was a miracle, but it was someone else's.

When I finished, he simply nodded, satisfied, and smiled. "A miracle," he declared. For him, that settled the matter.

I had no insight to offer, so I closed my eyes and yawned again.

"We'll have to get through security on the other end, too, won't we?" Sam asked after another moment.

"We will," I answered without opening my eyes. "Customs."

"I thought so. You . . . you may not see me when you wake up. But don't worry. I'll be right with you."

"I'm going to hire a car. And then I'll take you to Emily."

"I'll be right with you," he promised me. "Don't worry."

"I won't." I smiled as I sank slowly toward sleep and dreams. Sam had found what he wanted. I might not rank very high on the miracle scale, but I was exactly what he needed—I was enough, I was the one who could get him home for Christmas at last.

Just then, I realized something else. I'd found what I had been looking for, too, and satisfaction warmed me like a hug, or like light from a candle. I'd found an actual, true, honest-to-God original source for a real live genuine urban legend—if not for its beginning, at least for its end.

I'd found an original source, and it wasn't a co-worker's second cousin or a friend of a friend.

It was me.

12

Home For Christmas

he gentle bump of tires touching runway was enough to jar me from my slumber. When I looked over, Sam was gone. For a moment, I panicked. Had I been wrong after all? Had he vanished somewhere over the Atlantic, when the clocks in London chimed midnight?

But even as the thought occurred to me, I let it go. *No, he's not gone—just unseen.* Sam had promised that he'd follow me closely, and if there was one thing I'd learned about Sam, it was that he kept his promises. I didn't even look back as I deplaned and made my way to customs. I knew Sam's ghost followed behind me. We'd made it. Of course, I still had to find the hospital, find Emily's room, and smuggle Sam in, but I had no doubt I'd figure that all out when the time came. Faith, it seems, gets easier with practice.

At the terminal, I hired a car. *No, not hired, rented. You're on a different continent now,* I admonished myself. *It's rent, not hire, can, not tin, check, not bill, elevator, not lift, and for Heaven's sake stay on the right bloody side of the road!* The clerk at the counter gave me a map and traced out the directions to Piedmont Hospital. Which was good, because I'd forgotten to charge my phone.

A tram took me to the lot where I found my rental car. I opened the trunk and tossed my bag in and, after only a moment's disorientation, I climbed in on the correct driver's side. Sam was already there, waiting in the passenger's seat.

"Hi!" he said brightly. "Did you have a nice rest?"

Visiting hours were long past by the time we found our way through Atlanta's holiday traffic and arrived at Piedmont Hospital. Even at the late hour, the car park (no, parking garage) was nearly full. My stomach did unpleasant flips in my belly. Nonetheless, we soldiered our way in. Sam didn't pull his disappearing act this time; he hefted his duffle and followed close behind me.

The lobby was practically deserted. Only a single employee sat at the information desk reading a paperback mystery novel. Sam and I approached her.

"Hi," I said. "We're here to see Emily Prescott."

"I'm sorry," she said. "Visiting hours are over."

"Please," I said. "Can you at least tell me what room she's in? We've come a very long way."

"Are you family?" the woman asked.

Sam stepped forward and produced his military ID. "I'm Sam Prescott," he said.

The woman glanced at the ID and frowned.

Uh oh, I thought. *It's decades out of date!*

I looked around, nervously planning our escape route. But thankfully, the woman didn't call for security. She looked back at her screen, and the stern frown faded to concern.

"I'm sorry," was all she said. "You'll have to come back during visiting hours."

"But—" I began.

Sam interrupted me. "Pardon me, ma'am. Is there a cafeteria nearby? We've come all the way from London, and we'd like to at least have a quick bite before we decide what to do next." He smiled his most charming smile, and in that moment, I understood why Emily loved him.

"Down the hall to the left," the woman replied. "Y'all take the elevator down to the first floor. Don't drink the coffee. They stop making it fresh around five or six, and it'll be terrible by now. Take my word."

"Yes, ma'am," said Sam. "Thank you."

"Merry Christmas," the woman said, and she turned back to her book.

We followed her directions to the elevator. When we reached it, Sam pushed the button for the third floor rather than the first. I grinned. "Going snooping, are we?"

He nodded. "Can you work one of those machines?" He meant the computer the woman in the lobby had used.

Frankly, I had no idea. "We'll see." I didn't have a better idea. If we could somehow find Emily's room, we'd be ahead of the game. If we knew where we were going, it would just be a matter of sneaking in.

Yeah, that's all, right, I thought and felt instantly ashamed of myself.

Faith, Jessie, faith.

We left the elevator and hurried through the halls. It didn't take us long to find a nurse's station. At that late hour, it was empty. Taking a furtive look around to be sure no one was coming, I sat down at the computer terminal. The screen was dark, so I booted it up. No good. I slammed my fist on the keyboard in frustration.

"Is it not working?" Sam inquired.

"No. I need a bloody password."

"What now?"

"Let's see if we can find another one. Maybe someone left one on."

We tried two more stations, but the computers there had been shut down as well. A third was manned so we hurried past without making eye contact, hoping we wouldn't be stopped. *That's it, Jessie, just act like you know what you're doing.*

On the fourth floor we found a computer that was still on. There was half a cup of coffee on the desk that still felt warm to the touch, so I knew we had to work fast. I sat down and clicked away. It didn't help. I couldn't for the life of me figure out what to do. Nothing on the screen suggested a patient information database or anything of the sort.

"Jessie. . . ."

"I'm trying, Sam! Give me a minute. . . ."

"Don't worry about it," he said. "She's one floor up. Room Five-eighteen."

I turned my chair around. "What? How do you know?"

Sam smiled and held up a clipboard containing a supervisor's master list of patient charts. "*This* I can work," he said. "Come on!"

He hurried away and I followed him. When we reached the elevator, he pounded the up button a few times, then gave up and ran for the stairs. With his Emily this close after all the long years, he couldn't wait, not even for a second. I ran after him, taking the stairs two at a time.

We didn't run through the hallways on the fifth floor, but only because we didn't want to wake the sleeping patients or attract the undue attention of those whose job it was to keep us out.

Blast it! Why do hospital floor layouts have to be so bloody confusing? Why can't the stupid room numbers just run in numerical bloody order?

The fifth floor was even less crowded with hospital personnel than the one below, but even so Sam's uniform stood out like a Santa suit at a Jewish summer camp. We kept on looking straight ahead and moving with determination.

A thousand irrational doubts troubled my thoughts. *What if someone stops us? What if we have the wrong room? What if the door's locked? God forbid, what if we're too late? What if . . . what if Emily's dead?*

In the end, my worry didn't matter in the least. Faith prevailed. We found the right door. No one was about. My hand trembled as I turned the knob. It opened. Slowly, not daring to breathe, we slipped into the dark room and pulled the door closed behind us.

It took a few minutes for my eyes to adjust to the dim light. Emily slept in the narrow room's only bed. IVs fed nutrients and medication while an array of bleeping machines monitored her condition. She looked tiny, gray, and frail.

Sam beamed.

Moving quietly as a shadow, he dropped his duffle and slipped to her side. I stood silently by the door, my hand over my mouth and my eyes wide, as he pulled a chair next to her bed. She stirred at the slight sound and her eyelids fluttered.

"Hi, Em," said Sam. "It's me. Can you hear me, pretty girl?"

"Sam?" Her voice was fragile and soft, softer than a whisper. "Sam? It's you, isn't it?"

"It's me, Em." His voice broke. He was crying as he took her small hand in his. My own cheeks were wet.

"I always knew you'd come, Sam. I always knew. I waited for you, my dear. All these years, I never stopped waiting for you. . . ."

I didn't have to see Sam's face to hear the smile in his voice. "I promised you, didn't I, pretty girl? I promised. And here I am, home for Christmas. Though I guess this isn't exactly home, is it?"

"Home's where you are," Emily said.

And then I realized I was intruding. Sam had come a long way to be with his beloved. I didn't know how much time they'd have, but they deserved to spend it together. Tears were streaming down my cheeks as I let myself out, as silently as I could manage. I pulled the door shut behind me.

I'm not sure how long I stayed out there in that hallway, weeping with the exhausting and exhilarating joy of having witnessed a miracle. I sat down with my back against the wall and hugged my legs close to my body and I waited. There was an outlet there, so I started charging my phone.

Somewhere in the deep night, the sounds of commotion startled me. I looked up. People hurried by, ignoring me. I shook the sleepiness away from my head and stood, wondering what had caused the sudden tumult. Around the hallway corridor, I saw a small team of doctors and nurses rushing into Emily's room.

Oh my God, Emily!

Something was wrong. They must have been alerted by some change in the monitors that bleeped along with her weak and tired heartbeat. I stood and watched them work through the open doorway, but a part of me knew it would do no good. There was no sign of Sam.

I looked down at my watch. It was just after midnight, Christmas day.

The doctors did what they could. In the end, they stopped and bowed their heads.

After a moment, one of them shook her head sadly. "It's too late," she said. "She's still listed as DNR. Let her go gently."

It was over.

After a time, they left her. One of the doctors gave me a sad smile and a nod as he passed. And then, for a brief moment, I was alone with her. Emily's fingers were curled in death, as though they still held an invisible hand. She no longer looked pale; in her last moments a hint of color had returned to her cheeks. Her lips still held the memory of her last, peaceful smile.

But this wasn't Emily; Emily was gone. Like Sam said, this was only the shell, the dust, that which we leave behind. When Sam vanished, she'd gone with him. Wherever they were, they were together, together at last. Sam had kept his promise. They were home. They would be home forever.

I should call Roger, I thought after a time. *I should tell him he won't have to wait up on Christmas Eve anymore. I should tell him that Sam is a ghost of Christmas past now.*

After a few minutes, two men interrupted my vigil when they came to raise a sheet over her head. I lifted my hand to wave goodbye, and then I slipped away.

I thought about calling home, but I decided against it. It was late, and it would be more fun to surprise everyone in the morning anyway. Besides, I wanted a little time alone with my thoughts before I started the three-hour drive to Birmingham. I found a couch in a little waiting area at the far end of the hospital, so I took a seat, exhausted, at peace, wrapped in wonder. I'd just witnessed something amazing, and I needed a little time to process, to experience the power of the moment. I wanted to let the joy and awe of it all move and overwhelm me. I wanted to smile and cry and remember. I did all of those things. I stayed there on that little couch for a long time. It was a cozy spot and it had been a long time since I'd closed my eyes. At some point, I must have dozed off.

As I slept, I dreamed.

I was in the garden behind the little cottage where David's parents lived. I was standing on the little path and, just like on my wedding day, it was covered with flower petals. The air was heavy with the perfume of blossoms and growing things, and it was warm, warm like home at Christmas, and everything was washed in golden light. In the distance, I heard a melody of birdsong. Peace warmed me like a favorite blanket, and I could have stayed there forever.

As I walked, I heard another sound, or realized I'd been hearing it, and I tilted my head to listen.

There was music playing, music, gentle and laughing as a stream, and then I heard a voice, singing.

I turned, and it was David. He was singing, and his voice was low and soft, soft as a caress.

"Isn't it romantic? Music in the night, a dream that can be heard. . . ."

Before I could speak or even gasp, I felt his hand on the small of my back. He took my left hand in his, and then we were dancing, dancing, just as we'd practiced, and every step, every breath, was perfect. His hands were warm.

"Isn't it romantic? Moving shadows write the oldest magic word. . . ."

"David—" I managed. "How—"

"Shhh," he said. "Dance with me, my love."

And we danced. The song ended and another began, and another after that. We danced through them all, the first dance we'd never had, and our second, and all the dances after that. After a few more steps, I pulled him close and rested my head on his shoulder. I wanted to dance with him like that forever.

"Well," he said after a while. "This is it, eh? It's our hoedown hootenanny. How do you like it?"

I wanted to cry but I smiled instead. "I like it more than everything else in the whole world."

"I'm glad."

"Let's never stop."

"I'd like that," said David. "I'd like it more than anything. But I can't stay long. Your friend Sam opened the door for me, but only for a little while. At least we had our first dance. All the way to the end."

"Our last one," I said, trying not to cry.

"No, not our last," said David. "Never the last. But for a while. For now. Just for now. It's time to say goodbye, Jessie."

"I can't, David. I can't."

"Yes, you can, Jessie. I know you can. You have to, you know."

"I don't want to. David—"

"And hang our ornament, won't you? Our First Married Christmas ornament."

"I can't do that either." I was going to cry anyway. I didn't want to. I didn't want to cry for him. I'm such an ugly crier.

"Please, Jessie. For me. Hang our ornament and say goodbye. Okay? You'll do that, won't you?"

"I can't. I don't have it anymore. I . . . I threw it away."

I buried my face in his shoulder. I didn't want him to see me cry, not even in a dream. I couldn't see his face, but all the same, I could feel his smile. He smelled of salt and sandalwood, and a little like garden earth and damp wool.

"I love you, Jessie. I love you. I love you."

"I love you, David. I love you forever."

"I love you forever," he echoed.

I'm glad it was the last thing we said to each other.

I woke up alone. Time passed until I had no more tears left inside me, and, well, it wasn't getting any earlier. I was just about to stand and head back to my car when I happened to glance at the empty seat next to me.

And then.

Yeah, then. I'm not sure how to tell you what happened next.

I gasped, and my hands covered my gaping mouth.

Something was there, on the seat right there next to me. Something I'll swear wasn't there when I sat down.

It was a gift bag. A bag that looked . . . yes . . . oh, yes . . . *familiar.*

For the longest time, I just sat there, staring, wide-eyed, my mouth hanging open. I was afraid to look; I was afraid to touch it. I was afraid it would pop like a soap bubble and be lost, lost like dancing in a dream. For a long time, I didn't.

Then, with trembling hands, I reached for the bag. I opened it.

Inside, of course, was my Christmas miracle.

I lifted it out, smiling through my tears. It was the ornament, our ornament, our crystal Christmas ornament, pristine, perfect, unbroken, unbroken forever, with *First Married Christmas* written in neat, golden script.

It was a long time before I was ready to leave that couch. I'd still had some tears left after all, it turned out, and they came again. I was glad no one was there to see.

When I stood at last, I stumbled a bit. Looking down, I gaped again. *My foot hurt.* It was a very familiar hurt. I bent down and rubbed it. It hurt, almost . . . almost like I had a bruise. I smiled through the last of my tears. Even in a dream, David had stepped on my foot.

I took the bag with me, hugging it close to my heart as I stepped out into the clear, cold night, where all was calm and bright. I made it back to my rental car, limping only a little, and turned it toward the highway and Alabama. The gift bag with the ornament David had given me was on the passenger seat next to me, where I could reach out and touch it any time I wanted to. I did that a lot.

And so I drove.

I, the original source, the friend of a friend, the miracle, was going home, home for Christmas.

Y'all were all asleep when I got here, of course. I let myself in and put my stuff in my old room, quiet as a snowflake. Everything was the same, as if I'd never left it at all. I couldn't wait to sleep there again.

First, though, first I had something to do. I had a promise to keep.

I came back down, carrying my little gift bag with me. I hung the ornament on the tree; I knew you wouldn't mind. I hung it, just as I should have done long ago.

"Happy Christmas, David," I said when I'd found the perfect spot at last, the highest bough, just beneath the angel. "I'll hang it every year from now on. I promise. I love you. I love you. I love you forever. All the way to the end."

And then, with a deep breath, I said the thing, the thing I hadn't been able to bring myself say, the last thing, just as he'd wanted.

"Goodbye, David."

So. Here I am at last, sipping my coffee at home, with all of you, my sweet, precious ones, where I should have been a long time ago.

You see, I guess Mr. Longbottom was right after all. Sam's story had a gift for me. And he was right about something else, too. Sam's story is my story now. It's the story I've just shared with you, with all of you, my beloved family. This is my story, and this is how I've decided to tell it.

That, my dears, is the Gospel truth, every word, sure as I'm born.

About the Author

After a 30-year career in new media, where his titles included VP, Digital Media, VP, Creative, Executive Producer, and CEO, John Adcox is now concentrating on storytelling. In addition to his writing, he is the CEO of Gramarye Media, Inc., the "next generation" book publisher, game developer, and movie studio of the future. More of his books are coming soon. You can learn more about them at http://johnadcox.com/.

About the Illustrator

Carol Bales studies, works, and teaches in a place where technology and creativity intersect. Educated in painting at the University of Tennessee and Human-Computer Interaction at Georgia Tech, she works as a User Experience Researcher for The Weather Company and teaches at Georgia State University.

The couple lives in Atlanta, Georgia. They are the co-creators of *Raven Wakes the World: A Winter Tale*.